"GRACEFUL STORYTELLING . . . A FUNNY,
UNPRETENTIOUS DOMESTIC NOVEL."
—*New York Newsday*

"INVENTIVE . . . PUTS A WITTY FEMINIST SPIN ON THE
BROTHERS GRIMM." —*Ms. Magazine*

"DELIGHTFULLY LOONY." —*Booklist*

"TOUCHING AND FUNNY . . . ALWAYS ON TARGET."
—Associated Press

"A HIGHLY ENTERTAINING, ORIGINAL WORK, WHICH
GOES WHERE FEW WOMEN (OR MEN) DARE TO
VENTURE." —Laura Cunningham,
author of *Sleeping Arrangements*

"A WITTY, INNOVATIVE DEBUT." —*Publishers Weekly*

"WELL WRITTEN." —*Library Journal*

"FUNNY, INTELLIGENT, AND INVENTIVE . . . A MODERN-
DAY FAIRY TALE WITH AN IRREVERENT, FEMINIST
TWIST." —*Kirkus Reviews*

MARITA VAN DER VYVER lives in Stellbenbosch, South
Africa. *Entertaining Angels* is her first adult novel. Her
second novel, *Childish Things*, will be published by Dutton
in August 1996.

Entertaining Angels

Marita van der Vyver

Translated by Catherine Knox

A PLUME BOOK

PLUME
Published by the Penguin Group
Penguin Books USA Inc., 375 Hudson Street, New York, New York 10014, U.S.A.
Penguin Books Ltd, 27 Wrights Lane, London W8 5TZ, England
Penguin Books Australia Ltd, Ringwood, Victoria, Australia
Penguin Books Canada Ltd, 10 Alcorn Avenue, Toronto, Ontario, Canada M4V 3B2
Penguin Books (N.Z.) Ltd, 182–190 Wairau Road, Auckland 10, New Zealand

Penguin Books Ltd, Registered Offices: Harmondsworth, Middlesex, England

Published by Plume, an imprint of Dutton Signet,
a division of Penguin Books USA Inc.
Previously published in a Dutton edition.
Published in Great Britain by Michael Joseph Ltd.
First published by Tafelberg, Cape Town, 1992.

First Plume Printing, January, 1996
10 9 8 7 6 5 4 3 2 1

 REGISTERED TRADEMARK—MARCA REGISTRADA

The Library of Congress has catalogued the Dutton edition as follows:

Van der Vyver, Marita.
[Griet skryf 'n sprokie. English]
Entertaining angels / Marita van der Vyver : translated by
Catherine Knox.
p.   cm.
ISBN 0-525-93918-0 (hc.)
ISBN 0-452-27339-0 (pbk.)
I. Title.
PT6592.32.A517G7513   1995
839.3'635—dc20   94–27526
                                                            CIP
Printed in the United States of America

PUBLISHER'S NOTE
This is a work of fiction. Names, characters, places, and incidents either are the
product of the author's imagination or are used fictitiously, and any resemblance to
actual persons, living or dead, events, or locales is entirely coincidental.

For I. B.

All the characters in this novel are entirely fictional, as is proper in a fairy tale.

'The union of a frivolous form and a serious subject lays bare our dramas (those that occur in our beds as well as those we play out on the great stage of History) in all their terrible insignificance.'

Milan Kundera, *The Art of the Novel*

Contents

Scarey Tales

Riddle Tales

Dizzy Tales

Acknowledgements

The motto on page vi is from Milan Kundera: *The Art of the Novel*, copyright © 1988 Grove Press. Used with permission of Grove/Atlantic Monthly Press.

The mottoes on pages 1 and 143 are from the *Encyclopaedia of Magic and Superstition*, Macdonald & Co., London, 1988. The quotations on pages 136 and 139 are from the same work.

The quotation on page 4 and the first one on page 7 are from John Milton: *Paradise Lost*.

The second quotation on page 7 is from William Congreve: *The Mourning Bride*.

The quotations on pages 38, 89 and 109 are extracts from the Authorized Version of the Bible (The King James Bible), the rights in which are vested in the Crown, and are reproduced by permission of the Crown's Patentee, Cambridge University Press.

The quotations on pages 54 and 59 are from William Shakespeare: Sonnet 129.

The motto on page 69 is from Peter L. Berger: *A Rumour of Angels: Modern Society and the Rediscovery of the Supernatural*,

Scarey Tales

'Whatever else has changed on the continent of Africa, the deep-rooted belief
in magic, both white and black, has
not. Africans base their fear of witches
on the argument that somebody —
some person or spirit — has to be
responsible for the inexplicable.'

Encyclopaedia of Magic Superstition

I

Snow White Takes a Bite of the Apple

SYLVIA PLATH did it in an oven. Virginia Woolf in a river. And Ernest Hemingway with a pistol. Or was it a shotgun? Something phallic, anyway.

Quite funny, really, thought Griet. When women do it, it's obvious they want to return to the womb. The warmth of an oven. The waters of a river. The slow, lulling numbness of pills, like falling asleep.

But men commit suicide like they cook: dramatically and messily. Blowing their brains out, hurling themselves off skyscrapers, slashing their arteries. Blood and guts all over the place. No doubt because they know they don't have to clean up afterwards. There'll always be some woman to do that.

Anna Karenina did throw herself under the wheels of a train, Griet recalled. That could be pretty messy. But it was a male writer who made her do it. Shakespeare obviously understood women better than Tolstoy did. Poor Ophelia didn't fall on a sword like Hamlet, she floated peacefully away down a stream. And Juliet would have preferred poison but Romeo didn't leave her any – Shakespeare also seems to have understood men better than most other writers. So Juliet had no choice but to bleed.

Women actually don't like blood. Men might be less taken with it too, if they had to wash it out of their underwear every month, speculated Griet.

Even Snow White's ghastly stepmother chose a bloodless method of disposing of her husband's beautiful daughter. Though a masculine set of values lurks in the stepmother's style. In Western religion, the apple almost always symbolizes female sexuality. '*That fair enticing fruit*', which poor old Adam sampled, '*Against his better knowledge, not deceived, But fondly overcome with female charm.*' Snow White was punished for Eve's sins. And, like Eve, she was rescued in the end by manly valour. Snow White by a handsome prince on a white horse, Eve by an almighty god on a golden throne.

'I decided the oven was the only escape,' Griet told her therapist, who was watching her enigmatically, as usual. 'I don't know why, but that oven had fascinated me from the moment I moved into the flat. Probably because I'd never had anything to do with a gas oven before. Except in books and movies, of course.'

Rhonda's eyes were pools of innocence, blue and still. She looked as though she had never even heard a swear word. You'd never guess that she had to listen to other people's deepest and darkest perversions all day long.

Her hair was blonde and wavy and her hands lay still on the open file on her lap. Every now and then she wrote something in the file, as quickly and unobtrusively as possible, but Griet noticed every time. What had she given away about herself this time, she wondered distractedly, and it took quite an effort not to stumble over her next words.

'But ... but, as you know ...' Rhonda's gold pen scratched over the paper, the noise unbearably loud in the quiet of the consulting room. Griet drew a deep breath. 'Well, I thought I'd just see how it felt first, you know. Stick my head in without turning on the gas. Just to see if I'd be able to go through with it.' Rhonda wrote something in her file again. The second time in less than a minute, Griet realized in a panic. 'I ... well ... I knelt down in front of the oven, opened the door and slowly put my head inside, kind of turned sideways so that one of my cheeks rested on the wire rack.'

4

Sometimes Griet wondered whether anything would ever shock Rhonda. If one of her patients suddenly started masturbating in the consulting room, she probably wouldn't bat an eyelid. Nothing would ever trouble those blue pools.

'My head didn't fit in very comfortably – it's quite a small oven – so I opened my eyes to see how I was doing . . . No, I don't really know why I closed them in the first place. It just happened by itself, like my first French kiss at a school party. Maybe because I'd seen it done that way in the movies. Anyway, I opened my eyes – and looked straight at a dead cockroach! Right there next to me!'

Rhonda watched her, motionless.

'I couldn't believe it! I mean, I know my friend isn't all that tidy, and she probably didn't use the oven an awful lot, and I hadn't used it since I'd moved in – but a *cockroach*! I yanked my head out so fast that I banged it against the inside of the oven and collapsed on the kitchen floor. Half unconscious. Just imagine the humiliation if someone had found me there! Frightened out of my wits by a cockroach. I'd never hear the last of it. Anyway, when I eventually got over the shock and looked into the oven again – without putting my head right in this time, naturally – I saw not only a cockroach, but this thick layer of crumbs and hard-baked fat and God knows what else, all in there with the cockroach.'

Was she imagining it, or was there a hint of a smile at the corners of Rhonda's mouth? Impossible, she decided, looking away at the opposite wall. A yellow wall with a huge Mickey Mouse clock – the mouse's arms told the time; one arm was shorter than the other. The clock always seemed to hypnotize her as her sense of guilt grew with every movement of the mouse's longer arm. Children were going hungry while she paid a strange woman sixty rand an hour – *R30 a half-hour, R15 a quarter, R1 a minute, more than a cent for every second!* – to listen to her pathetic problems.

Rhonda's consulting room was as colourful as a

5

kindergarten classroom: red and yellow and blue furniture and mats and striped curtains. Probably to make her victims feel more cheerful, Griet had often thought. Armchairs that sucked you in like quicksand, so that only your head and knees were visible once you were seated. It was impossible to feel dignified if you could scarcely see over your own knees. It was like initiation at an Afrikaans university: a way of breaking down one's ego, only more subtle.

Rhonda never allowed an armchair to swallow her. Which made Griet all the more suspicious. Rhonda sat upright on a red sofa, her ankles neatly crossed. She wore linen slacks, a plaited leather belt, a gold Rolex. Griet was dressed in a multi-coloured frock, long and loose, and, as always when she was with her therapist, she felt creased and unkempt.

'And so I didn't commit suicide,' sighed Griet, twisting a wisp of untidy hair into a ringlet round one finger. 'I spent the rest of the evening cleaning the oven.'

'And how do you feel about that?' asked Rhonda.

Yes, she really was smiling. Griet sighed again and then smiled resignedly with her therapist. 'Well, I nearly suffocated in the fumes from Mister Oven. It must have been an ancient can. I don't think it had ever been used in that filthy oven. Maybe some chemical reaction or other took place, I don't know – something that made it poisonous. I wondered if anyone had ever committed suicide with Mister Oven . . .'

'You seem to have found some humour in the situation.'

'It actually wasn't very funny at the time,' Griet said rather sharply. 'I kept thinking about something Athol Fugard wrote somewhere, that he'd carry on making a fool of himself until the day he died, and then probably fuck that up too. Something along those lines.'

Rhonda didn't say a word.

'Yes, I know what you're going to say now. I'm still living through books and movies. Protecting myself from reality by pretending that I'm Scarlett O'Hara in *Gone with the Wind*.'

'Maybe someone a little more intellectual,' smiled Rhonda. 'How about the green-haired woman in *The House of the Spirits*?'

'She had blue hair,' Griet snapped, wondering whether her therapist wasn't right, as usual. 'And she was in *One Hundred Years of Solitude*.'

'See what I mean? You leap at the chance to discuss a fictional character. You come to me to talk about yourself and then spend half the time quoting from books.'

'But fictional characters are more ... I don't know, they're somehow more ... convincing.' Griet looked at the Mickey Mouse clock again. Five minutes more to go. That meant five rand – enough to buy a plate of food for a hungry child. Or three packets of cigarettes for herself. If she could only stop smoking! She sighed for the hundredth time in the last hour. 'I mean, have you ever read about someone who was saved from suicide by a cockroach? It could only happen in reality.'

Rhonda didn't respond, but her eyebrows lifted almost imperceptibly.

'Kafka wrote a story about a chap who turned into a cockroach, Gregor Samsa. The same initials as mine. And his sister also had a Griet-ish name. Gretel? Gretchen?'

It was time to read the story again, Griet decided. It had always been one of her favourites, perhaps because, in a way, the poor cockroach had also been killed by an apple. The apple his father threw at him, the one that wedged in his back. *The Symbolism of the Apple in World Literature*. Yet another ridiculous title for the literary thesis that she'd been postponing for ten years.

'*The fruit Of that forbidden tree, whose mortal taste Brought death into the world, and all our woe*,' wrote Milton. It was impossible to imagine Eve with a banana or a pear or any other fruit, for that matter. And it was an apple that caused the fall of Troy. The famous apple of contention that was thrown on the table for the most beautiful of three goddesses. Paris chose Aphrodite and the other two took vengeance. '*Heaven has no rage, like love to hatred turned*,'

William Congreve said, '*Nor Hell a fury, like a woman scorned.*'

'But even Kafka didn't write about a cockroach as a lifesaver. Snow White was rescued by a prince on a white horse – and Griet Swart by a dead cockroach in a dirty oven. Wouldn't you rather have been Snow White?'

2

Hansel and Gretel and the Struggle

'*THREE WEEKS* without a man', Griet wrote in her Creative Arts Diary, above her weekend shopping list. Wine, bread, butter, cheese, coffee, toilet paper and tampons – not necessarily in order of importance. This was one of the advantages of being manless, the abbreviated shopping list, with no shaving foam and chocolate for him, no vegetables and fruit for his children.

Tuesday 31 October 1989. Almost three months on her own, but three weeks without any contact. Without seeing him or ringing him or writing to him. She hadn't felt so proud since she'd managed to last three weeks without a cigarette.

There were close parallels. Her relationship with George did to her emotions what nicotine did to her lungs, she'd realized ages ago, but the relationship was as difficult a habit to kick as smoking. More than a habit – an obsession, a physical addiction, an oral fixation. One truly does keep all four seasons in one's groin, as she'd always teased him.

She'd enjoyed sex with George, more than with anyone before him. It wasn't an earth-shaking affair with shooting stars and similar celestial manifestations. It was playful, fun, funny and sometimes even absurd. If George felt adventurous and wanted to try an unusual position, he was sure to fall off the kitchen counter or bang his head on the edge of the bath or end up with a stiff neck instead of a stiff penis. George wasn't the acrobatic type, but sometimes he forgot the limitations of his own body and swept her along with him, and then they experienced a few moments of sexual trapeze before tumbling head over heels back to earth. Before the car seat became too uncomfortable or one of the children from his first marriage was roused by those strange noises coming from the dining room.

Not that George made many noises. Screaming orgasms weren't his style. And with the children in the house at weekends, Griet also had to learn to appreciate dark and silent sex. Like a blind-mute, she sometimes thought in a moment of rebellion.

Griet drank a cup of coffee on the balcony of her friend's flat, as she'd done every morning since moving in here. The street below came slowly to life. On the rickety plastic table lay the English-language newspaper, which she'd already scanned, the open diary with her shopping list, and a pencil for noting down her social commitments for the week. With a shock she realized that she didn't have any social commitments. Not a single date. The thought of yet another Friday evening on her own made her long for the comfort of an oven all over again. A clean oven, she thought before she could stop herself.

'It's dangerous to travel alone,' Griet wrote in her diary, 'specially after your thirtieth birthday.' It was All Saints' Eve tonight, she saw when she looked at the date again, New Year's Eve on the old Celtic calendar. The night of witches and goblins and other unholy spirits, the Scots believed. The blood of a Scottish sailor ran in her veins and she was by profession a weaver of fairy tales so she took the date seriously, but she was the only person she knew who still did.

The Americans had banalized it, as only they could, with children in silly costumes and candles in pumpkin shells. And Hollywood had converted it to cash, along with everything else that's supposed to be sacred, making a whole string of movies that consisted mainly of blood and screams.

Tomorrow would be the Day of the Holy Ones, Griet thought nostalgically, and the day after All Souls' Day when one was supposed to pray for the souls of the dead. There were a number of souls she should pray for: those from whom she had descended and those who had descended from her, her predecessors and her progeny. If only it weren't so difficult to pray.

She picked up the item she'd torn from the paper. '*One in five women heading Aboriginal households have told researchers that their stressful lives have driven them to attempt suicide.*' She attached the report with a paperclip to today's page in her diary.

Sex could become predictable after seven years with the same man. But it was a comforting predictability, like a well-loved poem that you read over and over again until you knew it off by heart, until nothing but a punctuation mark could still surprise you. Until one day you look at a comma as though you've never seen it before. She knew the language of her husband's body as well as she knew her own tongue, the salty taste of his navel, the bony hollows on his shoulders, the stickiness at the tip of his penis. And yet she still sometimes discovered something – perhaps a mole – that she'd never noticed before. Her body was at ease with his, under his, on top of his.

She had sometimes seen shooting stars, but it'd been light years ago, when every night with him was still a satellite voyage of discovery. They'd married three years ago and on the nuptial bed such heavenly appearances became as infrequent as Halley's Comet. She was always pregnant; her poor husband touched her less and less. Month after month his gloom increased and his playfulness faded. *The Incredible Shrinking Penis*, that's what she'd call the story of her marriage.

Maybe it was the story of every marriage.

She took another sip of coffee from her friend's cracked Arzberg cup, contemplated smoking her first cigarette of the day, decided to resist the temptation, and stared with unwilling fascination at the newspaper report under the paperclip. '*They revealed that they had to bear the brunt of "the whole Aboriginal situation", including recurring problems of unemployment, alcohol, imprisonment and racism.*' Count your blessings, Griet dear, Grandma Hannie always said.

Once upon a time there was a woman who came from a dreadful family, she wrote on the clean sheet of paper before her. One of her grandfathers was in the habit of talking to angels and the other grandfather believed in ghosts. She was perhaps a witch, perhaps a rebel angel, undoubtedly a troublemaker, and she was sorely punished for her sins.

The worst of all her sins was using words to seduce people. She was a woman who wanted to play with sentences like Salome played with her seven veils. She was a woman who wanted to write because she believed that the pen was mightier than the penis.

She didn't realize that this was the eighth deadly sin in a phallocentric world.

She wasn't barren like so many other sinners in so many other fairy stories. Pregnancy came easily to her, time after time, but each time she had to hand her child over to death. She could conceive and she could carry a baby, but she could not give birth to one.

After four pregnancies she was still childless.

It was such a terrible punishment that sometimes, like the goose girl of long ago, she wanted to climb into an oven in protest against her fate. But these days it isn't so easy to climb into an oven. And you can no longer count on a hero to come and haul you out, either.

It was time to go to the office, Griet decided, listening to the increasing drone all round her. It was an indescribable noise, the sound of an animal waking up, as though the mountain, to which the city clung like a tick, was stretching its back and flexing its muscles. She snapped her Creative Arts Diary shut and got up to fetch her handbag from the bedroom floor where it lay amid magazines and newspapers.

She'd ask someone to join her for a drink on Friday

night, she decided, banging her empty coffee cup down on the sticky kitchen counter. Anyone, she decided as she locked the door behind her.

She missed sex, she realized with devastating certainty on this All Saints' Eve morning. Even Halley's Comet was preferable to the total eclipse of the moon under which she'd been trying to survive for the past few months.

She missed her husband, she missed her house, she missed the predictability of Friday nights with him and his children. Michael and Raphael came every weekend and she'd cook for them and they'd eat while they watched TV – *MacGyver* and the news and *Police File* and a film – and she'd clear away the empty plates and her husband would doze off on the sofa and she'd take the boys to their bedroom and pull the bedding up so high only their eyes peeped out and she'd laugh at the faces they pulled every time she kissed them goodnight. She might be crazy, she thought defiantly, but she missed it.

It was Rhonda who'd suggested she write about it.

'But no one wants to read about a failed marriage,' she protested. 'Not in this country. We've enough other problems.'

'Write it for yourself,' said Rhonda, phlegmatic as always. 'Not for other people.'

'You mean like a diary?' Griet turned up her nose as though she'd been confronted by a blocked drain – an all-too-frequent occurrence in her friend's flat. 'I'm a bit past that.'

'No, I mean like a story. Fictionalize yourself. It's what you're always doing in your imagination anyway.'

Griet had laughed off the suggestion – or so she thought. But it must have stuck somewhere in her subconscious. Once upon a time, not so long ago, there was a woman. That was her first thought when she woke up this morning. Who on earth still began a story with 'Once upon a time'? That was her second thought, as she sat up with the taste of the previous evening's last illegal cigarette like a reproach on her tongue. It was her work that was affecting her mind, she decided for the umpteenth time.

She earned her bread and butter at a publisher's, in an office full of children's books, at a word processor on which she edited and translated and sometimes fabricated fairy tales and other fantasies. The last year or so she'd been busy with what would probably be the most comprehensive collection of fairy tales ever to appear in Afrikaans. It was a strange experience to be taking stories that had been passed on orally for centuries and pinning them down by pressing a bunch of electronic buttons in space-age characters on a personal computer. Magic meets technology.

I know what magical realism is, she often thought. Her clever friends were quick to talk about it, but she rediscovered it afresh every day at her word processor. The South Americans didn't have exclusive rights to absurd situations and anachronisms.

'Why do they call it a personal computer? The only personality that mine has ever revealed is a ruthlessly psychopathic streak,' she told her therapist after a particularly demanding day at work.

'So, you think your computer doesn't like you?' Rhonda asked, serious as always.

'Now you're making me sound paranoid again,' Griet accused her. 'No, that isn't what I'm trying to say. But only a psychopath could take a story you'd poured your soul into for weeks and tear it to shreds before your eyes, then throw it into a fire without any compunction. That's how it feels when your PC wipes out a story.'

Her clever friends said machines didn't have human characteristics. But you couldn't always trust your friends. Her friends fell into two groups – the clever ones and the mad ones – and she dangled in mid-air somewhere between them, struggling to get her feet down on to the ground. The clever ones were in law or journalism or academe and they liked talking about politics and religion and the latest French film with subtitles. They sat in stylish restaurants sipping vintage wine from crystal glasses and argued about Namibian independence and Wimbledon tennis. Their feet were always firmly on the ground, even when they were drunk. The mad ones were painters and writers and other artists who sat at home smoking dope and drinking boxed plonk out of cheap glasses while they quarrelled about the Struggle and erotic art and people's culture. They sometimes got high on pills or other substances, but they always came down with a painful bump the next morning.

'Mandela reminds me of Hansel who was caught by the witch,' she confessed to her friend Jans during one of many lengthy restaurant meals. 'You know, the one who had to stick his finger through the bars every day so the witch could feel if he was fat enough to slaughter.'

Jans was a lawyer with a political conscience that compelled him to work for the Struggle. It had landed him in a moral dilemma because he was making a packet out of the Struggle. He'd bought a cottage with yellowwood floors and a fireplace, but he felt so guilty about so much luxury that he gave the key to his less privileged black friends every weekend and hiked off into the mountains. And he liked reading myths and legends which he wouldn't discuss with anyone but Griet.

It was George who'd started the speculation about Nelson Mandela's seventieth birthday in the Victor Verster Prison – while he topped up everyone's glass with sparkling wine. Anton-the-Advocate and Gwen-the-Journalist had dived into the conversation with the eagerness of children who wanted to prove they weren't scared of the deep end. Gwen's lover, Klaus, reckoned that not one of the liberals round the table would recognize Mandela if he walked into the restaurant now. Not even a radical like Jans. The only photographs they'd seen of him were nearly thirty years old. And, as usual, Anton's wife, Sandra, looked as though she was trying to listen telepathically to her children at home in case one was crying.

'Oh, that Hansel,' said Jans.

'I hear he has his own sickbay where he's examined twice a day by a major from Prison Services.'

'Hansel and the witch?'

'Mandela and the major,' said Griet.

Jans smiled and wound a long ribbon of pasta deftly round his fork. Klaus told the rest of the group about an article on South Africa he'd read in *The Economist*.

'And you think he needs a Gretel to push the witch into the oven?'

'Maybe – but remember, Hansel didn't wait passively for Gretel to come and rescue him.' Griet had cut her own pasta into pieces and was carefully loading her fork. 'He was too clever for the witch. He didn't really stick his finger out.'

'He fooled her with a little stick!' Jans laughed and took a great swig of sparkling wine. 'And you think Mandela is fooling them?'

Griet shrugged. 'I can only hope he remembers the fairy tale.'

The Struggle, thought Griet as she made her way to her office full of children's books, the eternal Struggle. She'd often tried to convince Jans that fairy tales were nothing less than people's culture. Stories handed down from the people for the people. The same crystal-clear division between good and evil – princes and dragons, black prisoners and white warders, fairies and witches, township kids and suburban housewives – the same simple presentation, the same moral lessons. But to sit and spin fairy tales all day didn't give her much credibility in the Struggle.

Tonight she'd throw her balcony door open wide, Griet decided while she waited at the traffic lights across the street from her office block, and she'd fly away with the wind. Ring-a-ring-a-roses through the clouds, over the sleeping city with a fork and a spoon, leap-frogging over the curve of the moon. Up, up, up on to the flat slab of the mountain, where the witches were sure to meet on All

Saints' Eve. Round this giant table under the moon, with a lion and a devil keeping guard at each end. Who'd dare to chase them away? Not even the angels.

3

In Search of the Golden Goose

THE WOMAN – witch, rebel angel or ordinary sinner – lived in a dreadful country. The sun always shone, except at night when the moon shone, and the people of the country changed colour like loaves in an oven. From creamy-white to biscuit-brown to coffee-black, or from salmon-pink to beetroot-red, or from the colour of butter to the colour of turmeric. Some even from blue to green. But the worst sinners never changed colour. They just bleached whiter and whiter.

This is what Griet had written on a sheet of paper in her office full of children's books that afternoon. It seemed a long, long time ago, she thought with her chin in her hand and her elbow on a bar counter. She'd crumpled up the page and rung her friend Jans: 'How about joining me for a drink?'

'What's the occasion?'

'It was the Day of the Dead yesterday.'

'Can't we be like ordinary people and just have a drink because it's Friday?'

'But it's a feast day in South America. The Mexicans buy sugar-bread skeletons and lay a place at table for absent guests. They believe it's the day the dead get leave in heaven to visit the earth again.'

'I can't think of a better reason to drink myself into a stupor.'

'OK, Jans, it's Friday evening, I've survived another week on my own, and if you don't have a drink with me, I'll beat you to a pulp next time I see you.'

And now, several drinks later, she remembered there was something important she wanted to tell him, but she couldn't think what it was. Her head felt like a flower that was too heavy for its stem.

'I've had a gutful of clever men,' she muttered into her hand. 'I'm looking for a stupid man. Stupid and strong.'

Jans looked at her blankly through the round gold-rimmed spectacles that had slipped down on his nose. He was still in his working clothes – a conservative dark suit, white cotton shirt and muted paisley tie – but the top button of the shirt was undone and the tie had been tugged loose. If Jans didn't have to wear a suit every day, Griet had often thought, one could easily mistake him for a fairly decent tramp. He always looked as though it was two days since he'd last shaved, and three days since he'd combed his hair. And to crown it all, tonight he looked as though he hadn't slept for four days: his mouth was tired and there were shadows like bruises under his eyes.

'I don't mean the village idiot, Jans. He'll have to be able to read and write. I don't trust men who don't read. Maybe that's the root of my whole problem. Instead of checking on whether he likes dogs, as my mother always said I should. Or what his underpants look like.'

Her sister Petra was a connoisseur of men's underpants. Said they spoke volumes. Never trust a man with holes in his underpants. She didn't really like red underpants either. Said it was a dictator's colour.

'But I look at his bookshelf,' sighed Griet.

'If he reads Camus, he's OK?' A light seemed to have been turned on behind Jans's spectacles.

'Something like that, yes.' Griet took another sip of wine and shook her heavy head. 'And I land on my bum every time.'

'We aren't just talking about George and the recent past?'

'No, we're talking about men in general, the whole catastrophe. I've never had a decent relationship with a man who didn't have an overload of intellectual pretensions. Of course, this says a lot about my own intellectual pretensions. But the best one-night stand of my life was with a gym instructor who'd never read anything heavier than the back page of a Sunday paper.'

That was a long time ago, of course, when she still shaved her legs regularly. If he could see her now with a dowdy ponytail and all her lipstick smeared off on to the wine glass, clinging to a bar counter, the poor gym instructor would completely lose his impressive erection.

So this, then, was what people did on a Friday evening. There had been a time when she also went out on Friday evenings, when she still wore mascara and flirted with muscle-bound instructors, but it must have been in a previous life.

'Just say you could have lived with him?' Jans stared at the rows and rows of bottles behind the counter, endlessly reflected in sparkling mirrors, an alcoholic vision of heaven. 'How long could you have stood it before you started screaming every time he opened his mouth?'

'For always – if I'd known what I know now. The problem with clever men is that they talk too much and don't screw enough. The trouble with stupid men is usually the same. But every now and then you find one who knows how to shut up and use his body. Then you must hang on to what you've got – and bite your tongue every time he says something stupid. But that's what you have to do with any man, anyway.'

All men are the same in the light [Louise wrote from London]. Graffiti that I read in the tube on my way to work. But I never seem to see the light, let alone a man in the light. It's dark when I go to work in the morning and dark when I come home again in the evening. This is definitely going to be the winter of my discontent, here in the country of Shakespeare and the Sex Pistols where I always wanted to live. It's terrible when your dreams come true.

'But I'm a sucker for a clever man. I always think maybe he's an Einstein or a Shakespeare and then I could be his muse. Behind every man, you know; all those clichés I was brought up with. Immortality by proxy. I believed George was a genius. A philosophy lecturer – how lucky can a girl get? I felt like a bird-watcher who'd come across the last dodo in existence. And then I discovered he didn't want a muse, he wanted a mother. Someone to darn the holes in his underpants.'

'Perhaps that's part of a muse's role,' Jans said comfortingly while he tried to catch the waiter's eye and order another bottle of wine.

'No, there's a world of difference between a muse and a mother.' She pushed her glass towards him so he could take a mouthful of her wine in the meantime. 'You can't convert your muse into Florence Nightingale. You can't expect Shakespeare's dark lady also to play the lady with the lamp.'

'You can't have your cake and eat it?'

'No, you can eat as much cake as you like, but you can't expect a chocolate cake and a custard tart to taste the same.'

Griet began to shake with laughter and realized that she'd had enough to drink. But she raised her wine glass resolutely, drained it, and felt herself waft away on a cloud of recklessness. Jans was looking more and more attractive, with his spectacles low on his nose and that dark shadow of stubble round his mouth.

'You know, just the other day I read something about a flower that made me think of you,' said Jans. 'Have you ever seen a *wildemagriet*? An ox-eye daisy?'

'Do you know the story of the sad princess?'

'It's a beautiful flower, but very poisonous.'

'Her father said that the man who made her laugh could have her hand in marriage.'

'The black people believe it brings protection against the devil.'

'And it made you think of me?' asked Griet and started to hiccup in wonderment.

'I thought that would make you pay attention,' laughed Jans. '*Callilepis laureola* is its botanical name.'

'Hell, Jans, this is why I like you,' hiccuped Griet, flopping down on her elbows. 'You're a minefield of useless information. I always wonder when the next explosion is going to get me.'

'There's no such thing as useless information,' insisted Jans, refilling her glass. 'You never know when it'll come in handy. Who made the sad princess laugh?'

'The bumpkin with the golden goose,' replied Griet, still hiccuping. 'Don't you remember, the goose with a whole row of people stuck to it?'

She remembered a Friday night, long ago, when she and George flirted in a pub. There was a guitarist playing the same songs over the same din: 'Imagine', 'Streets of London', 'Where Do You Go To, My Lovely?'. Maybe it was the same pub.

The next morning they woke up in the same bed.

She could hardly believe her eyes. She couldn't explain how it had happened. She enjoyed his company, but she wasn't sexually attracted to him. She was unusually impressed by his bookshelf. That was the only excuse she could come up with for her behaviour.

'And now?' she asked, quite at a loss. 'What now?'

'What do you suggest?' he laughed, folding her in his arms. 'Do you want to get married?'

She laughed with him, touching his body in amazement. He was thinner than he seemed in his clothes, more defenceless. He had a slight paunch, narrow hips, long legs. And a penis as soft as down and warm as a chicken, stirring at the touch of her fingers. She wished she could play with it all day without having it grow hard in her hand, but there wasn't a good fairy nearby to make her wish come true.

Disappointed, she felt the chicken transform itself into a bantam cockerel. Why does a man always think he's letting a woman down, she wondered, not for the first time, if his penis doesn't leap to attention the moment she touches it?

'I'm not going to fall in love with you,' she warned him.

'I've been in love with you for ages,' he answered. But she thought he was teasing again.

'Well, don't say I didn't warn you. I don't want a steady relationship. I'm not ready yet . . .'

'Hush,' he'd said and kissed her so she couldn't protest any further. 'You'll make me impotent if you don't shut up.'

Prophetic words; Griet thought, years later. She never became his muse. She married him and drove him to impotence.

'You hold me too tight at night,' she told him that first month. 'I'm not used to it. I get too hot, it feels as though I'm suffocating.'

'You'll just have to get used to it,' he laughed. 'I can't sleep empty-handed.'

'You never hold me at night,' she reproached him years later. 'I may as well be sleeping alone.'

'I can't hold someone at night,' he answered. 'It makes me feel claustrophobic, I can't breathe.'

'I don't want to be a man's muse any more,' she told Jans, who was becoming blurrier, as though she was looking at him through a camera lens that was being turned more and more out of focus. 'I am looking for a man who is stupid enough not to get impotent if he becomes my muse. Or don't you get male muses?'

'Originally they were the Greek goddesses of the arts, but these days everything is so androgynous that the sex of muses probably doesn't count for much any more.' Sometimes she thought that Jans was only interested in mythology because most modern people regarded it as useless information. 'And if he refuses to become a muse, you can always make him your Pegasus.'

'Wasn't Pegasus a horse?'

'Exactly. The winged horse of the muses. Inspiration for the art of poetry. As in: I mount my Pegasus. Means I'm going to write a poem.'

'I like that,' laughed Griet and hiccuped louder than ever. 'Let's drink to Pegasus.'

'To the bumpkin with the golden bird.' Jans raised his glass in yet another toast. 'May you find him soon.'

4

Goldilocks Loses Her Spectacles

ONCE UPON a time there was a colourful land that was regularly struck by disasters. There were long droughts during which thousands of animals perished; there were flash floods that washed thousands of houses away. There were earthquakes that destroyed historical villages like the Finger of God flattening pawns on a chessboard, and there were man-made laws that had the same effect. The difference between the natural catastrophes and the man-made disasters was that the people left churches and mosques and other religious buildings standing, like kings without subjects on the deserted chessboard.

The worst disasters in the colourful land were always caused by people. There were mountains that spewed fire, not because a god decreed it should be so, but because careless people set the mountains alight. There was a dangerous hole in the air above the land through which the sun's deadly rays shone down and burnt man and beast. The hole wasn't made by a god either, but by people who were more concerned about holes in their clothes than a hole in heaven. What the people didn't realize was that the angels watched them through the hole, like children lying on their stomachs, peeping through a crack in an attic floor. And the angels were so shocked by what they saw that their wings bristled on their backs.

It was a country where black rhinos and black children perished by the thousand. Then one day the people grew concerned and collected millions of rand to save the rhinos. It was without doubt a strange land, the angels told each other, shaking their heads.

'I'm writing a fairy tale,' Griet told her therapist. 'I actually wanted to write about my relationship. But I'm better with fairy tales.'

Rhonda smiled encouragingly, a teacher watching a toddler forming her first letters with clumsy fingers. She must have had a trying day, reckoned Griet, because there was an unmistakable crease in her long cotton skirt. But her blouse was as snow-white as ever. Not even a grimy ring in the collar. Griet smoothed her own blouse self-consciously. It had also been clean this morning.

'Do you want to tell me more?'

'No,' Griet said quickly and then added apologetically, 'There isn't really much more to tell. I've hardly begun. I don't know how it's going to end.'

'*Nuns startled by green ice from heavens*', she'd read this morning in the paper, one of those absurd little reports she always remembered better than the serious main stories. She obviously had a need for inexplicable phenomena, after seven years with a man who could explain everything logically, rationally and unemotionally. And any question he couldn't answer, like what is the meaning of life, he could always evade with cynicism.

A large piece of green ice, she read with increasing interest, had fallen out of the air through the window of a Roman Catholic convent. The nuns, frozen in terror, had stored the evidence in a fridge.

Evidence for what? Griet wondered. A court case against the divine powers that had hurled the ice earthwards? And who would stand accused in the dock? The angels surely wouldn't take out their disappointment in the human race on a group of nuns. No, Griet decided, the poor witches would probably get the blame again. And how could you hold it against them if they broke a few convent windows now and then? Everyone knew what the Roman Catholic Church had done to witches for centuries.

'Have you seen George again?'

'No.' Griet glanced at the Mickey Mouse clock. Still almost a full hour to go. She might as well be honest. 'I tried to see him. I drove past our house a couple of times . . . I mean his house . . . or past friends' houses where he might be visiting. But I couldn't pluck up the courage to go in. I'm afraid of what I might do to him.'

'Are you still angry with him?'

'I don't want to beat him to death like a month ago, if that's what you mean. I'll never be stupid enough to try to hit him again. I nearly broke my hand. I don't even know how to make a fist. It just isn't something that decent girls learn at school. All we ever learnt was how to kick a guy in the crotch, but the PT teacher said that's very serious and you should only do it if you're being raped.'

Rhonda nodded sympathetically, but didn't say anything.

'She didn't say what you should do when your baby dies and your husband drives you out of the house,' said Griet.

'You were very badly hurt.' Rhonda leant forward a little on the red sofa, her eyes peaceful, as always. Griet felt as though she could sink away into those still pools, down, down, down, with stones in her pockets, like Virginia Woolf. 'And you hide it under this terrible anger.'

She didn't want to beat him to death any more, she told her therapist. She wanted to torture him to death slowly, but she didn't tell anyone that. She wanted to lock him into his own house, without a telephone or newspapers or books or any contact with the outside world. She wanted to flush his sleeping pills and his depression pills down the lavatory. She wanted to install a remote control video camera in every room, and watch him as he slowly went mad.

Sometimes her own madness frightened her.

'He says he can't understand why I'm so angry. That's

the worst of all, that he can carry on with his life as though nothing had happened, as though I were a page that could simply be torn out. Not a page with words on it, not something you'd miss if it disappeared from a book, not even a bloody advertisement page! A snow-white, completely blank page.'

'Isn't it perhaps possible that you want to punish him in some other way now?' Rhonda asked carefully. 'Now that you don't want to hit him any more?'

'How do you mean?' Griet asked, just as carefully.

'Didn't you think about him the night you put your head into the oven?'

'I knew you'd ask that,' said Griet slowly.

Grandpa Big Petrus, who'd been punished with the Hand of Death, often spoke to the angels. That was long before there was a hole in heaven, but he had his own methods of making contact with celestial beings. He'd simply take a long walk in the veld, look up into the cloudless sky of his beloved Karoo, and hear the fluttering of angels' wings.

He agreed with them that he lived in an extraordinary country. Specially after he'd lost his farm during the depression years and had to live as a poor relation on his nephew's farm. People said he never got over the humiliation, it had affected his mind, he'd started hearing voices. But little Griet knew that since childhood he'd talked to the angels like other children play with fairies and gnomes. He told her himself, when she was still very young and he was already very old, one day while she was listening to the fluttering of wings with him.

'He was a good man,' Grandma Hannie said after his death, 'but he was too proud to be a poor relation. That's why he was punished with The Hand.'

Grandma Hannie always spoke with great awe of The Hand.

'He was meek and mild,' Grandma Hannie always said. 'He only got angry once in his life. Then he struck a man stone dead. He didn't know his own strength. The magistrate said he'd been punished with The Hand of Death and he might never again strike anyone, not even his own children.'

Grandpa Big Petrus was a giant of a man – so big that Grandma Hannie had to make all his clothes for him. He had feet like mountains and hands like hills. Little Griet couldn't keep her eyes off his hands, specially not that deadly one that had sent a man straight to his grave with one blow. The Hand was as brown as the earth and baked rock hard by a merciless sun, cracked like an empty dam in a drought.

Grandma Hannie was a tall, sinewy woman with long sinewy hands, but when she knelt beside Grandpa Big Petrus, he folded both her hands in one of his. Grandma Hannie's hands were covered with blotches and blue veins that always made little Griet think of villages and rivers on a geography map. But Grandma Hannie's fingers were light as feathers when she dried Griet's hair.

'My prettiest sister died of wet hair,' Grandma Hannie always told her. 'She had curly golden hair like yours, only much longer, almost down to her knees. She washed her hair every day, and sat brushing it in the sun for hours. Like a mermaid, the people always said. One evening she got caught in the rain and she went to bed with damp hair. The next morning she was lying in bed with her hair wound round her body like a golden cloak. Stone dead.'

Grandma Hannie was the youngest of sixteen children who had all come to bizarre ends.

One brother broke his neck when his horse shied at a ghost one night. It must have been a ghost, people said, because he was the best rider in the district. He wouldn't have fallen off his horse, even if he'd been drunk.

It was the ghost of the sister with the wet hair, the family whispered. She was taking revenge because he'd snipped off a tress of her hair after her death. He'd apparently wanted to give his daughter a doll with real hair.

Another brother had married seven wives – sometimes more than one at a time, went the gossip – and suffered a heart attack on his seventh wedding night. The bride was a good forty years his junior, and six months later she gave birth to a child who inherited all his money and, according to the chagrined family, didn't look like him at all.

But the strangest death of all came to the brother in the tower. He'd ended up the richest of all – because he was the stingiest, Grandma Hannie always said, but money couldn't buy him happiness, she never failed to add. Never a very cheerful soul, in old age he gave himself over to gloom completely and built a tower that soared up to heaven on one of his farms. He sat in it all day scanning the horizon, on the lookout for the Communists or Judgement Day, whichever came first. One day he heard the roaring of lions and the trumpeting of elephants and decided Judgement Day had dawned. The Communists wouldn't bring elephants along, he reckoned. He hurried down but, in his haste, he tripped on the tower stairs and broke his neck.

The elephants and lions belonged to the first circus that had ever toured the district.

Griet thought about her family, that night she wanted to get into the oven, and wondered whether committing suicide like this wasn't awfully unoriginal.

'I probably thought about George too. But I was fed up with always considering other people, what they'd say, how they'd feel. For once in my life I wanted to think of no one but myself.'

'But you couldn't do it,' said Rhonda carefully. 'You couldn't do it because you were still thinking about other people.'

'I couldn't do it because a cockroach gave me a fright.'

'I know it's going to sound strange to you,' said Rhonda, writing something in the file on her lap, 'but the fact that you considered suicide, considered it seriously, but didn't go through with it . . . indicates a degree of progress.'

'*Progress?*'

'Up until now you have simply hidden behind anger, Griet. You refused to accept any responsibility for anything that happened. Now you're beginning to face reality. That's the most difficult part. It's understandable that you would sometimes think about suicide.'

But I think about suicide all the time, she wanted to argue. I think obsessively about suicide and cancer and starving children and about what the hell is going to become of this country if heaven doesn't help us. I have anxiety attacks about death and the possibility of getting Aids – maybe I already have Aids! – and that I could be raped or necklaced by a furious black mob, and then I think what the hell, if I do it myself at least I can choose the way I go. What's finished is finished, Grandma Lina always said.

But suddenly she felt too tired to argue with her therapist.

'Can you remember how you felt that day? Did something happen, no matter how slight, something that could have been the last straw?'

She hated it when her shrink sounded like an article in *Cosmopolitan*.

'Yes,' she answered crossly. 'My spectacles fell off.'

'Pardon?'

'The day I put my head in the oven.'

A slight disturbance swept across the blue pools, a ripple stirred the water, and Griet smiled.

'*As soon as you stop waiting for him and focus attention on yourself, life will improve no end*', she'd read half an hour earlier in Rhonda's waiting room. '*Show me a fairy tale with a beautiful woman in it and I'll show you a bimbo in limbo waiting to be released by the love of a good man.*' She'd snapped the magazine shut in irritation and lit a cigarette.

She craved a cigarette now, but she'd forbidden herself to smoke in Rhonda's consulting room. A person had to have some self-discipline.

'It was as though I had always looked at life through the proverbial rose-coloured glasses – such a wonderful hazy world – and then the glasses suddenly fell off. And then, for the first time, I saw myself as I am. Not as I'd like to be. It was a hell of a shock.'

'Help Me Rhonda', the Beach Boys sang, 'Help Me, Rhonda'. It was a tune that often ran through Griet's mind when she looked at the Mickey Mouse clock. Her hour was nearly over.

'It finally got through to me that maybe I'd never have a child, never write a great novel, never even have a successful relationship with a man. I'd never felt so fucking useless before.'

'You spent nearly seven years with a man,' said Rhonda comfortingly from her red sofa. 'You were married for three years. You can't make out now that everything was one big disaster.'

'Sorry,' mumbled Griet, 'but that's how I feel. It's like a movie with a bad ending. You remember the end, no matter how good the rest was.'

It was not clear why the ice was green. That was the last sentence of the report she'd read that morning, the sentence that had given her hope again. At least there were still some things that even her husband and her shrink couldn't explain.

5

And Why Are Your Eyes So Big, Child?

THERE WERE days like today, when Griet felt as though she was trapped in the middle of a massive children's party. Every woman in the supermarket had a child hanging on to her hand or packed into her trolley among the groceries. As though you could buy a child off the shelf like a life-sized gingerbread man.

And as if the epidemic of children weren't enough, every shelf in the supermarket mocked her failure as a woman. Baby bottles and disposable nappies and Purity food in various colours and flavours. Toddlers' toys and pet food, colouring books and fat crayons, peanut butter and golden syrup. Everything made her think of children.

On days like this she envied the biblical Sarah. Or Lorca's Yerma. They'd at least escaped the humiliation of the modern supermarket.

Purposefully, she walked past the rows of medicine, past Kiss-it-better-with-Band-aid and the Doctor-it-with-Dettol, heading for the boring washing powder aisle. She felt like Little Red Riding Hood – in a red T-shirt with an orange plastic basket – who had to resist the temptations of the forest. Her only comfort was that she didn't have to push a heavy trolley round since she no longer shopped for her husband and his children.

It was impossible to explain how everything in her

contracted every time she thought about the children she'd lost. Four of them: three from her husband and, long before she met him, the first one, which she'd chosen to get rid of. And now the two stepsons too. Half a dozen children, four from her own body and two from her heart, all lost to her.

She couldn't even discuss it with her shrink.

She chose the cheapest washing powder because the advertisements all sounded the same to her. Idiotic women who took greater pleasure in clean washing than in sex. *Can you see the difference?*

She wasn't sorry about the abortion, she'd decided again and again. She hadn't thought of the foetus as a person. She hadn't given it a name.

But she wondered, since she'd lost the others. She wondered whether she was being punished because she hadn't wanted that one. And she was angry with herself because she couldn't shake off the fetters of Calvinism.

Good Lord, she'd been twenty years old, what could she have done? Her poor partner in crime had been barely a year older – the first man she'd ever slept with, fancy that! A sunburnt blond boy on a surfboard. It was a catastrophe that would ruin her promising student years, her brilliant career, her whole golden future.

She'd never told him she was pregnant. She still saw him round town sometimes – a successful businessman in a silver-blue BMW, married with two children – and wondered what he'd have done if he'd known. She wondered how many men all over the world would never know that their lovers had had abortions.

It was difficult enough to share birth with a man, to make him understand how it felt to be ripped open in such a primitive way. It was almost impossible to share an abortion with a man.

Take Louise, for example. Her lover had dropped her in a back street in Woodstock, pressed a blank cheque into her hand and wished her good luck. He only pitched up at her flat again three days later. Griet's sister Petra was another case in point. Her lover had driven to Lesotho with her and stayed in a hotel with her until she stopped bleeding, but their relationship was over within a month. You just can't win, Petra had wept. There was no such thing as a successful abortion. Something always had to be sacrificed.

Griet walked past the pet products and looked away quickly when a picture on a tin of dog food caught her eye. Beware of the wolf, Little Red Riding Hood's mother had warned her, keep an eye open for anything that looks like a wolf. Griet had wanted a dog very badly – something to cherish in place of a child – but her husband wouldn't hear of it. Beware of men who don't like dogs, her mother had warned her.

Of course she believed in a god, she had argued with her cynical husband. You can't believe in witches and angels unless you also believe in a god. But her god was a god of love, not a wicked wizard who punished you because you'd had an illegal abortion as a twenty-year-old student. Her husband believed in nothing; not in wizards, not in gods, not even in himself.

She liked to think the first one had been a boy. She knew the next two were girls. She'd given them names, Nanda and Nina, and spoke to them for hours on end. Warned each of them against wolves and men who don't like dogs. Funny how you recall your mother's least sensible advice when you have a daughter of your own. You'd do anything to protect her: tell her she mustn't go to bed with wet hair; ask a good fairy to make all her wishes come true; sell your soul to the devil if it would buy her happiness.

But it hadn't helped. She'd carried each of them for only three months. The only proof that they'd ever existed was the sonar pictures of two foetuses, no bigger than Thumbelina, the fairy child.

She walked past the meat fridge. Maybe she wouldn't feel so bloodthirstily angry with her husband if she became a vegetarian. She hesitated near the coffee. Maybe she wouldn't feel so sexually frustrated if she stopped stoking her libido with caffeine. She chose a bag of Blue Mountain filter coffee and placed it resignedly in her plastic basket.

She found it amazing that she could get by without caffeine, nicotine or alcohol whenever she was pregnant. As though her whole body was working so hard to create a human being that there was no energy left for unhealthy obsessions. The maternal instinct must be one of the most powerful forces on earth, stronger than any army, more potent than witchcraft or technology. Stronger and more potent – and less comprehensible – than even mankind's self-destructive urges.

The fourth one was the son who'd stolen her heart. And no wonder! He'd spent a full nine months creeping closer and closer to her heart, until, near the end, she could hardly breathe at night. He was too lively for the space in her womb, it seemed that he wanted to invade the space round her lungs too, as though he regarded all the inside of her as his territory. His birth left her body empty, a house without furniture, a kitchen without an oven.

The birth was an agonizing experience that dragged on right through the night, worse than her worst nightmares. 'Is it possible that an apple could cause so much trouble?' she asked the young nurse who was holding her hand. 'Do you think Eve deserved such a heavy punishment?' The nurse smiled like an angel, rose up above the bed and floated out.

Maybe she was hallucinating, maybe her grandfather had sent one of his angels to hold her hand. She'd thought she'd be brave – her great-grandmother, after all, had borne sixteen children without the help of painkillers or modern medicine. But after a couple of hours Griet begged her angel nurse for relief. An epidural, a gas mask, a Caesarean, she mumbled, anything to get her out of this hell.

The fairy tale of South Africa, her bedevilled brain remembered, also began with an Eve. An Eve and a Mary, as in the most famous fairy tales of the Western world: the

Old and the New Testament. Eva was a Khoi-khoi girl, adopted by Jan van Riebeeck's household, as innocent and almost as naked as the original Eve. Maria de la Queillerie had travelled far with her husband van Riebeeck, 'founder' of 'white' South Africa, like the other Mary, to save a sinful world.

That's the European version, anyway, the white woman aiding black sinners. Like any good fairy tale, this one also has various versions, white and black and brown and yellow. Like Little Red Riding Hood and Rotkäppchen and Le Petit Chaperon Rouge.

A short while after the anaesthetist had inserted a needle into her spine, her legs started to grow numb and lifeless. And her brain, thank heaven, a little clearer. But she couldn't get poor Eve out of her mind. The Eve she'd learnt about at school, the one who was banned from Paradise as punishment for her sins. But also the other one, the one of whom she'd learnt no more than a name in class. The one who married a white man and was banned to Robben Island for her sins.

The Khoi-khoi Eva became a practising Christian, wearing Western clothes, learning to speak Dutch and Portuguese, and married the gifted Danish surgeon, Pieter van Meerhoff. But after the wedding the fairy tale went awry. Eva's husband died a few years later and she became an alcoholic and a prostitute, leaving her children to the mercies of charity. She was held on Robben Island several times, and died there in 1674.

So much for happy endings, thought Griet, and then the angel said she must push.

At last she pushed her baby out, ecstatic – in spite of the blood and the sweat – as though he was the saviour who would redeem mankind. He was her saviour, the child she'd waited for for so long, the son she wanted so badly.

She saw the slippery little body, the tiny feet with ten perfect toes, the pink face with eyes tightly closed against the savagery of the world. This is how it must feel to see a god, she thought.

And then they took him away. She could not weep when they told her he was dead. There was just an emptiness in the place where her heart had once beaten.

An Italian woman of ninety-one, Griet had read in the paper this morning, was reunited with her son who had been adopted shortly after his birth seventy-four years earlier. 'I wanted to find my son before I died,' Assunta Rabuzzi had apparently told reporters. Griet immediately snipped out the report and fastened it into her Creative Arts Diary.

She tried not to think while she did the rest of her shopping. Little pork sausages that reminded her of her son's toes; button mushrooms that looked like his nose. Shell pasta that imitated the perfect curves of a baby's ear; downy peaches that felt like a baby's skin, bringing a lump to her throat as her teeth broke through the skin of the fruit, making her weep with longing while she gulped down the chunks. '*Take, eat; this is my body.*' Once, long ago, on her grandfather's farm, she'd seen a sow eat her own piglets. Then she'd gone behind the sty and brought up her grandmother's lunch.

In a trolley in front of the dairy products sat a little boy with wide grey eyes. She'd ignore him, Griet decided, taking a block of butter for her basket. He was wearing blue canvas shoes and swinging his feet. Griet wondered what sort of cheese she should buy, and where the child's mother was. Mozzarella.

Why did her favourite newspaper reports, like her favourite foods, usually come from Italy? Green ice falling on convents and ancient women finding lost sons. Pizza and pasta and Parma ham. Maybe foods like this make the mind more susceptible to fantasy and outlandish stories.

She could hardly imagine what boerewors and biltong did to the minds of her own people.

In Dante's vision of hell, the souls of suicides are portrayed as stunted trees beside a river of blood. Imagine how many South African trees must be growing beside that blood-river! All the men who'd destroyed their families before they committed suicide, as though they were afraid that no one but their own children would play with them in hell. All the political jailbirds who'd flown out of tenth-storey windows, and all the others who'd pre-empted the authorities and taken death into their own hands.

Just imagine whom she might have met in this grove of stunted trees if she hadn't been frightened off by a cockroach. Griet felt her feet lifting off the ground. Hemingway and Hitler, Janis Joplin and Marilyn Monroe, Othello and Ophelia . . . Griet rose slowly, watching the child's swinging feet grow smaller and smaller. Nat Nakasa and Ingrid Jonker . . . It was dangerous to leave little boys like this in supermarket trolleys, she realized while she hovered high above the fridges full of cheeses from different countries. Van Gogh of the Netherlands and Cleopatra of Egypt and the chaste Lucretia from classical Italy . . . Mad people could easily steal them. She wafted through the ceiling, as easily as the winged horse of the muses would glide through the clouds. She flew, free as a witch, light as an angel.

6

I'll Huff and I'll Puff and I'll Blow Your House Down

GRIET FELT like crying when she saw the house she'd lived in for so many years. Home is where the heart is, she thought as she walked through the neglected garden. And if you no longer have a heart, home is probably where your books and your music and your most precious memories are kept.

The clivias burnt like orange flames under the bedroom window. A powerful antidote to impotence, according to old wives' tales, and protection against evil. Although a small forest of clivias couldn't protect the inhabitants of this house from impotence or evil.

She unlocked the front door carefully, and felt her knees weaken as she stepped inside. She could smell her husband, she realized in a panic in the hallway, next to the table with the telephone and the answering machine. But he couldn't be here. She'd made certain that he wouldn't be here. It was only his smell lingering in the house: the smell of his toasted cigarettes and his body after a game of tennis and the red soap he used every morning in the shower. She could smell him because the memories in this house sharpened all her senses, because she had crept back like a dog to dig up old bones.

Grandma Hannie's house was a House of the Senses, a

small labourer's cottage on a Karoo farm, cool and dark as a cellar, specially on Sunday afternoons when everyone was supposed to be sleeping. There was a front door used by nobody but the *dominee* and a back door that stood open day and night with a screen door that slap-slapped continually. One hard slap, deafening until you grew accustomed to it, and two softer slaps like echoes, every time someone came in or went out of the kitchen.

There were a number of other noises around the house, specially on a hot Sunday afternoon. The crack of the dog's jaw as he snapped at flies, the complaints of the windmill in a sudden gust, the drone of a lorry far, far away on the highway. The creak of Grandpa Big Petrus's bed when he rolled his giant frame over.

And at night there were inexplicable gurgling noises in the attic. Grandma Hannie said it was rats or something; Grandpa Big Petrus said: Impossible, rats don't gurgle, it was Something. Grandma Hannie shook her head and held her peace.

The most memorable sound was the hymn they sang in their bedroom at dawn each day, after they'd read a passage from the Bible and said a few prayers. Grandpa Big Petrus's confidently pure bass, followed by Grandma Hannie's hesitant falsetto. She didn't care much for singing, she only did it to make him happy.

Griet looked through the pile of unopened mail on the telephone table, found a few envelopes addressed to her, mostly accounts that she thrust into her handbag and Reader's Digest Sweepstakes which she crumpled up. She went to the kitchen to throw them away. Really just an excuse to postpone braving the bedroom.

She'd left in a hurry, just throwing a toothbrush and a few items of clothing into a suitcase, in the middle of the night after her husband had told her she was the most pathetic specimen of humanity he'd ever come across. She'd spent the rest of the night sitting in her car down at the beach, feeling just as pathetic as her husband said she was. At five the next morning she'd gone to her office – the security guard in the entrance foyer stared at her creased clothes and uncombed hair – and rung Louise in London.

'I need your flat for a couple of weeks, until I find a place of my own.'

'What's wrong?' Louise mumbled drowsily – it was still dead of night in London. 'What's going on?'

'George has thrown me out.'

She tried to sound businesslike, not to saddle Louise with her personal problems, but her voice wouldn't co-operate. The night in the car had been unreal, a nightmare she'd wake from, but now she was awake. She didn't have a fairy godmother, she told herself in front of her word processor in the grey morning light. She couldn't think of anyone capable of turning a pumpkin into a flat.

'Shit.' Louise's usual response to any communication out of the ordinary. After a long moment of silence during which Griet expected the dreaded 'I told you so', Louise sighed dramatically, 'Marriage stinks, that's all I can say.'

'Can I use your flat, please, Louise?'

Her voice was trembling dangerously.

'Of course.' Louise was wide awake now. 'Stay as long as you like but don't be surprised if I join you in a couple of months. My husband's driving me up the wall.'

Louise had married a British citizen because she wanted to get rid of her South African passport – as she admitted unblushingly – but she was sceptical enough about the arrangement to hang on to her Cape Town flat. You never know, she said. It's best to keep the back door open. She'd learnt her lesson with her first divorce. Griet thought her friend was far too cynical to make any marriage work.

'Is it that bad?'

'It's like being married to the Pope. And not being able to tell him he doesn't have any clothes on.'

'That was the emperor.'

'No, the fucking Pope! It's the righteousness that gets me down, the holier-than-thou attitude that Brits like him are apparently born with. He won't even fart in front of me. As though only we barbarians from Africa have such basic needs. But when he's in the shower, he farts so loudly I can hear him in the living room.'

'Where's he now?'

'Don't worry, he still doesn't understand a word of Afrikaans. Anyway, I just wanted to let you know that you're not alone in the struggle. Marriage is a great institution, as they say, but who wants to live in a fucking institution?'

Despondent, Griet got up from the phone and again passed the confused security guard. It was going to be a miserable day, she thought while her car lights sliced through the wisps of mist that hung low over the quiet streets. Welcome to reality, Louise had said.

And now, three months later, she was still in limbo. Alone in a strange flat with a kitchen full of cockroaches.

When other people split, she thought as she squirted the hole in the ozone layer bigger and bigger in her Struggle against the cockroaches, the man is normally the one who moves out of the house.

The woman is after all the one who looks after the house, she thought resentfully, who's responsible for everything from the colour contrast of the living-room cushions to the choice of toilet paper. Not always because she *wants* to be responsible for everything. Sometimes she's just too tired to make a feminist last stand in front of the stove. Anyway, Griet acknowledged bitterly, it's humiliating to wipe your bum with newspaper while you and your husband argue about Germaine Greer and Gloria Steinem. In the end it's less trouble simply to go out and buy the toilet paper yourself.

But everyone knows it's easier for a man to live out of a suitcase. What do you do if you begin menstruating in the middle of the night and you discover you didn't pack your Lil-lets? Or if you forget your imported nightcream and you don't have enough money to buy another jar and every morning when you face a borrowed mirror you have to stare in horror at the new wrinkles that have formed round your eyes overnight?

What is a house without a woman? Griet wondered as she walked through her house for the first time in weeks. What is a woman without a house? What is a woman without her husband's razor? She'd always used George's – infuriating him – to shave her armpits. He didn't like hairy women. Of course she could have bought her own razor during the last three months, but somehow she hadn't got round to it.

You're the only woman alive at the end of the twentieth century, Louise had written to her last week, who still believes that frogs turn into princes. And now you're disillusioned because the opposite happened. So what, Louise wrote. Join the club.

Griet wished she could be as cynical as her friend. But she wanted to cry over her house that felt as abandoned as an Afrikaans church on a weekday. She stood in the kitchen where she'd never been plagued by cockroaches and stared moodily at the unwashed clutter in the sink. Mostly glasses, she noticed, wine glasses and whisky glasses and almost all the other glasses in the drinks cabinet. It looked as though her husband had had a party every night since she left. Or was drinking himself to death in remorse, she thought hopefully.

For a moment she contemplated turning on the tap and doing the dishes, but she managed to stop herself in the nick of time. It was too late to play the kind fairy now. As if he'd ask her to come back if he came home to a clean kitchen tonight.

It didn't look as though he was eating much. There were only three plates in the sink. In the fridge she found a dozen cans of beer, a couple of bottles of wine, a box of milk (sour: she sniffed against her will), a heel of mouldy cheese and four eggs. She wondered what the children ate when they came for the weekend. She wondered whether there was toilet paper in the bathroom. And whether he'd remembered to pay the telephone account in time and water the rosemary bush near the back door regularly and to leave a window open at night for the neighbour's peripatetic cat.

It had nothing to do with her any more. She'd only come to get clean clothes and a couple of books, she reminded herself. She suddenly noticed that he'd removed all her photographs and postcards from the pinboard next to the fridge. It's fucking final, she realized, and fled blindly from the kitchen.

In the bedroom she could smell him again, the unlikely combination of sweat and soap and smoke. But she didn't smell another woman, thank God. She wouldn't have been brave enough to cope with that. Not while her own smell still lingered in the corners.

Grandma Hannie's house had always smelt of food, of baked bread and stewed quinces, and sometimes also of animal carcasses on the butcher's block. The smell of blood always took Griet back to that house. That was where she'd smelt her own blood for the first time, on the day of Grandpa Big Petrus's funeral.

Symbolic, she thought afterwards, but at the time she hadn't seen anything symbolic in the situation. Just the cruelty of fate to choose the day she had to wear a lily-white funeral dress. The family thought she wouldn't stand up in church to sing with the congregation because she was so heartbroken. Shame, the local women whispered sympathetically, she was the apple of her grandpa's eye.

She left the church after everyone else, thankful and relieved that the dress was still unstained.

That night she felt that her life was over, as though she'd been buried along with her grandfather. She was still thirteen, just like yesterday, but suddenly she had to behave like a grown-up. Tomorrow she'd have to sit with the women in the kitchen, sweating under the strips of yellow fly-paper that dangled from the ceiling, while the other children squealed in the farm dam.

She tossed and turned and was roused from her uneasy

sleep in the early morning by the saddest sound she'd ever heard. Grandma Hannie was singing a hymn, her reedy voice quite out of tune without her husband's lead, but determined to soldier on alone. '*On mountains and vales, the Lord is o'er all . . .*' Somewhere, Griet thought, Grandpa Big Petrus was smiling satisfiedly. And it was only then she could weep for his death for the first time.

Griet looked longingly at the double bed, the heart of the house, the hub that her life had turned on for seven years. She and her husband had never sung in their bedroom. She'd inherited her grandmother's tuneless voice and her husband preferred philosophizing to singing. He believed it was only emotional Italians and sentimental Germans who liked to sing.

Griet yanked the wardrobe open, suddenly in a hurry, and threw a bunch of hangers on to the bed. She had to get out of this house as quickly as possible and never come back. It was like Pandora's box, the memories that crept out all over from the moment she'd unlocked the front door. It was worse than Pandora's box. Pandora had at least kept hope.

7

The Grandmother Who Was Afraid of Everything

GRANDPA KERNEELS grew up near the sea. You could hear the sound of waves in his blood, Grandma Lina always complained, when he lay sleeping at night. For Grandma Lina, who was terrified of water, it must have been torture to spend every night beside a man who sounded like a giant seashell.

If the Good Lord had meant us to swim, Grandma Lina often said, He would have given us fins. Grandma Lina cited the will of the Good Lord for everything she didn't want to do. If He had meant us to fly, He would have given us wings. If He had meant us to be educated, He would have given us bigger heads. If He'd meant us to go and live on the moon . . . and so on.

Six weeks without a man, Griet wanted to write this morning in the book she'd bought on the way to her office. But the book was so pristine, with its gentian-blue cover and pages like starched collars and a quotation from a famous woman on every page, that she couldn't desecrate it with such a predictable first sentence. The paper looked as though it'd been handmade, the sort that had you wishing you could immortalize your thoughts in calligraphy. 'We don't see things as they are, we see them as we are', stood above Anaïs Nin's name on the first page. 'I was always a sucker for a beautiful book,' Griet wrote under these wise words, 'even more than for a clever man.' Nearly as bad, she realized too late, as 'Six weeks without a man'.

Then she turned the page and started to write about her grandparents. She'd actually bought the book to write about her relationship, as her therapist had advised her to do, but her story simply chose its own course like a horse that refused to obey its rider. All she could do now was to close her eyes tightly, hang on for dear life and hope that she wasn't thrown off like Grandma Hannie's poor brother.

Pegasus could obviously get by without a muse, but what happened to a muse if she was thrown off by Pegasus? A horse didn't need saddle and bridle, but a story needed a beginning and spelling rules and punctuation and an ending. If I can't even control a little filly of a fairy tale, Griet asked herself in a panic, how am I ever going to tackle a full-blooded novel?

Grandma Lina wasn't only afraid of water, but also of lightning and germs and illnesses, and the dark and death, in roughly inverse order of importance. If she heard the rumble of thunder – fortunately a rare occurrence as she spent her entire life in the Cape Colony – she covered all the shiny things in her house. It was a formidable task because everything in her house shone. Even the floors gleamed like mirrors. But she got to work with gusto.

She drew the curtains and threw sheets over the mirrors and even hid the bathroom taps under facecloths. And while the lightning played eerily round the house, she inspected the kitchen like a drill sergeant to make sure that no spoon nor fork ventured forth from a drawer to attract the destructive impulses of a bolt of lightning. While this was going on, Grandpa Kerneels would be out in the garden admiring the spectacle, a sublime *son et lumière* offered free to earthlings.

Grandma Lina's battle against darkness and death began all over again every evening immediately after sunset. Each night she left a light burning somewhere in the house but never the same light two nights in succession. She believed the globes would last longer if they each had a turn to rest regularly. She closed all the windows and locked all the doors and ensured that her whole house was spotlessly clean. There was always the possibility that she'd lose the battle, that she'd die during the night, and her soul would never rest at peace if someone could say she'd been a slovenly housewife. She washed her feet one last time and pulled on a pressed nightdress and lay down on her back with her hands folded on her breast – the only position in which she was prepared to die – and then tried vainly to fall asleep.

And the following morning, like every other morning, she was amazed to find herself alive.

'I've lost control,' Griet had admitted the day before in her therapist's consulting room. 'I can't even write about what I want to.'

'No, you have the reins firmly in your own hands.' Rhonda's Rolex flashed gold as she made a subtle inscription on her lap. 'You are writing about what you want to, even though you don't realize it. Remember we're dealing with the subconscious here.'

'No, it isn't . . .' Strange that Rhonda also used a riding term, she thought. 'Why would I want to write about my grandparents?'

'Because you don't want to write about your relationship. Because you still refuse to accept that it went wrong.' Rhonda was wearing long white linen trousers again, with a powder-blue button-through shirt, as cool as an umbrella on a hot beach. 'And that you also had a part in the break-up.'

'But what has a fairy tale about my family got to do with my relationship?' Griet snapped.

'It helps you to understand yourself,' Rhonda answered calmly, as though she hadn't picked up the irritation in Griet's voice. 'Like any proper fairy tale.'

'What do you do if you feel off balance?'
'I go and talk to a therapist.'

Grandma Lina was actually the sort of woman who should only exist in washing-powder advertisements, Griet wrote in her new notebook. To have the whitest sheets in the street was a matter of life and death to her. Life is not too short to soak your table napkins in Jik, Grandma Lina believed – every single day.

Sometimes she woke in a fright in the middle of the night, soaked in sweat, because she'd dreamt of a dirty mark on the kitchen floor or a film of dust on the top shelf of the wardrobe. She couldn't get back to sleep before she'd been down on her hands and knees to check the floor or up on a chair to inspect the wardrobe. Sometimes the insomnia was so bad that she spent the whole night ironing.

She lived in a simple suburban house, exactly the same as all the other houses in the street, but for Grandma Lina it was a palace. Her husband was the king and she was the queen, germs and dust her lifelong enemies, and the broom and scrubbing brush her loyal subjects. There was a small garden with a birdbath in the middle of a small fishpond (an out-of-character concession to the king who loved water) and geraniums and dahlias beside a concrete path. There was a drawing room with a very upright piano and a Tretchikoff painting (the orchid on the steps) and a display cabinet full of ashtrays with place-names on them. There was a bedroom that smelt of mothballs and a toilet with green tiles that smelt of disinfectant and a kitchen that smelt of chocolate cake and red jelly.

Outside the kitchen was a polished stoep with a wooden bench and a backyard with a fowl-run and a giant fig tree. Grandma Lina could stare at that fig tree for hours while she stood before the window washing up, or sat at the table polishing her knives. Her gaze was always fixed on the lowest branches.

Grandma Lina had a thing about that fig tree. Little

Griet could have sworn that one afternoon she had seen her grandmother up among the leaves. Many years on she was still wondering whether it could have been merely a trick of her imagination, until Grandpa Kerneels made a remark one day about grown-ups who climbed trees. Grandma Lina glared at him and hurried out of the room.

Then Griet knew that her eyes hadn't deceived her. Her worthy grandmother was a secret tree-climber. You'd never guess it, of course, if you saw her in that serviceable day-dress and worn shoes, with her dark hair always neatly plaited and twisted tightly against her head in a bun.

Griet could only begin to understand years later. In the fairy tale about the king's son who was afraid of nothing, there was an apple tree – what else? – that the hero had to climb to pick an apple. As soon as he'd done this, he could do anything.

Climbing trees was Grandma Lina's only defiance of fear. From early childhood, she'd always preferred to hide in a tree than play with the other children. A lovely girl with dark hair and dark eyes, she was shy and nervous and obsessional. Too dark to be completely white, some people said, but in those days it wasn't such a scandal as it would be after 1948. School was a nightmare for her. If a teacher asked her a question, she stuttered and stammered and sometimes even dissolved in tears. When an inspector visited the class, she began to tremble so badly that two children had to hold her desk steady. When she was in Standard Eight her father decided she was too sensitive for further study. And, anyway, the local pharmacist wanted her to come and work for him.

The pharmacist was a middle-aged widower with an eye for a pretty girl, and her father knew only too well that his dark daughter was one of the prettiest in the whole district. What the pharmacist did to her, Grandma Lina would never say, but she never forgave her father. Like a prince on a white horse, a man as blond as Grandma Lina was dark, Grandpa Kerneels arrived in the nick of time to save her from marriage to the middle-aged widower. They were wed within a month – the handsomest couple ever seen in the town – and they went to live in the city where Grandpa Kerneels could smell the sea.

Three nights before Grandma Lina died, she woke in a fright and sat bolt upright, but not because she'd been dreaming of germs. She'd heard someone knocking on the back door. Although she was normally too nervous to open the front door to anyone even in broad daylight, she didn't shake Grandpa Kerneels awake that night. She got up quietly, tiptoed to the kitchen and opened the back door.

Who or what she expected, her descendants would never know. The backyard was enclosed by a high wall topped with spikes of broken glass and rolls of barbed wire. It was impossible for any mortal to get to the back door from outside.

But Grandma Lina had got up as though it were the most natural thing in the world that someone should come and knock on the back door in the middle of the night and she should get up and open it. When she found no one there, she went back to bed. Grandpa Kerneels woke up when she came back.

'I heard someone knocking on the back door,' Grandma Lina told him matter-of-factly, 'but there was no one there.'

Grandpa Kerneels immediately suspected foul play and didn't close an eye the rest of the night.

The same thing happened the next night. This time Grandpa Kerneels woke up when she got out of bed. She'd heard the knock again, she said quite calmly, except that it sounded more as though someone was hammering on the door now. Once again Grandpa Kerneels had heard nothing, but he went with her to the kitchen to see what was going on. Once again there was no one. Grandpa Kerneels inspected the backyard for an intruder, letting the beam of his torch play over the fig tree and every possible and impossible hiding place.

The funny thing was, he said later, Grandma Lina had dropped off to sleep again immediately while he, normally a sound sleeper, lay awake for the second night in succession.

The third night, when Grandma Lina sat up suddenly, he knew she'd heard the knock again.

'It sounded as though someone was trying to break the door down,' she said, still not looking the least bit worried or frightened.

'It was only a dream, dear,' he tried to comfort her. 'I didn't hear a sound.'

But off she went by herself to open the back door, as though she'd never been afraid of anything. When she wasn't back after ten minutes, Grandpa Kerneels went to look for her.

She was lying under the fig tree on her stomach, spread-eagled. The last position in which she'd have died if she'd had a choice. A heart attack, Grandpa Kerneels said, or a stroke.

But no one else in the family ever saw the corpse. Griet always suspected that Grandma Lina had fallen out of the fig tree, and that Grandpa Kerneels had decided to bury her secret with her. She would have preferred it that way. To fall out of a tree in the middle of the night would simply seem too undignified in a death notice or on a grave-stone.

'It just goes to show,' Grandpa Kerneels was still saying years later. 'She didn't believe in ghosts and omens and things like that. She said only a fisherman could be so superstitious.'

8

Sleeping Beauty Fights Insomnia

SEX IS definitely a problem, Griet decided. And masturbation isn't a solution. '*The expense of spirit in a waste of shame Is lust in action*', Shakespeare wrote four centuries ago. A waste of shame, and Shakespeare wasn't even a Calvinist.

She lay sweating in the darkness, the sheet clinging to her naked body. These days she was wearing a nightie again – pale blue with a frill round the neck, bought while she was pregnant, chaste as when she was a child. But tonight was one of those humid summer nights, almost sub-tropical, when you knew that you were living in Africa. Where for centuries people hadn't been too bothered about clothes.

And because she was naked tonight, she thought about sex. Calvin's bequest to her people hadn't made things easier. Was it coincidence that *lus*, the Afrikaans word for lust, could also be translated as a noose? *Give them enough lust and they'll hang themselves?*

She'd pulled up the blue blind at the window, hoping that sometime tonight a breeze would play over her skin. Like a man's hands, she thought longingly, fingers caressing her hips and thighs, making music with her body. She touched herself, stroking her stomach, tangling her fingers in her pubic hair, feeling the gooseflesh break out. But it wasn't the same. It would never be the same.

The moonlight shining through the open window made the room look otherworldly. Moonlight is supposed to be silver, but that's just another modern myth. If you're tossing and turning, burning in frustration without even the smell of a man, moonlight is grey – blue-grey, lilac-grey in some patches.

Masturbation was still a taboo subject, Griet told herself as she contemplated her body in the moonlight. Even among her friends who had no scruples about discussing sex. If they talked about the Lonely Deed, they retreated into the past tense – as though it were the preserve of schoolchildren, like smoking on the sly – or behind cynicism and mockery. A woman needs a man because a vibrator can't push a lawn-mower, ha ha ha.

Was it because you did it on your own that there was so much shame attached to it? There weren't many swear-words left for the last decade of the twentieth century, but 'alone' had to be one of them. 'Alone' and 'Aids', Griet had realized since she'd been trying to live without a man. To be single was to be a misfit among all the couples around you. It was nothing short of perverse.

She let her hands slide down to her groin, allowed her fingers to stroke the secret skin on the inside of her thighs. The softest, shyest, sweetest skin on a woman's body, George always said. From here it was only a tongue's length to the heavenly hors-d'œuvre, the angel on horse-back, the muse on Pegasus.

Her male friends all acknowledged that they'd masturbated at school. In every thinkable and unthinkable place: in biology classrooms, in cinemas, even in team competitions in hostel bathrooms. While the girls sitting near them in those biology classrooms and cinemas – the poor respectable girls like Griet – didn't have the faintest notion that wanking was by far and away the most popular sport among their male classmates.

It was something that she often envied men, the easier relationship they had from early on with their sexual organs. Masturbation could at least familiarize you with the map of your own body before you risked the frightening, uncharted territory of the opposite sex. But for Griet and all her respectable sisters, sex was a double-track road from which you strayed more or less accidentally on to the single track of masturbation, not the other way round.

Griet was an adult woman before she first ventured to that mysterious region 'down under' by herself. It shows you what becomes of respectable girls, she thought later. It takes an awfully long time before they learn to fly on their own.

Griet was prim and proper at school, hardly aware of her private parts except for the three days of the month when she was fed up because she couldn't swim with the boys. When the penny finally dropped and she became aware of the powerful attraction this Forbidden Territory held for the opposite sex, she guarded it with the vigilance of a crack commando. These days she wondered whether it had all been worth the trouble, all those years of desperate defensive tactics, in dark cars and on uncomfortable sofas, to keep that virgin membrane inviolate – only to give it over to the enemy of her own free will in the end.

Like South Africa's vain attempt to hold on to Namibia. Or the Soviet Union trying to separate people with a wall. Nowadays Griet accepted that you can't cordon off a geographical area in an artificial way, not even your own body.

Her hand was cool against the feverish warmth of her groin. She rubbed her ring finger lightly over her clitoris, drew her middle finger up to the hollow of her navel, spelled out her hunger with an index finger on her stomach. Then she let the witching finger sink slowly down to where she'd grown moist with longing.

As an inhibited schoolgirl she hadn't been able to thrust even the smallest of Lil-lets – 'designed by a female gynaecologist for safety' – into this secret opening. The thought of anything bigger or harder – like a finger designed by a male god – threw her into paroxysms of anxiety. A male sex organ would definitely be a fate worse than death.

What do you do, she'd wondered, panic-stricken, if you get stuck? Two dogs could be dragged to the nearest tap, but two people?

And when she finally laid down her arms at the feet of that young surfer who was riding the waves of success in the business world these days, she was almost disappointed that everything went so smoothly. A few drops of blood later she began to suspect that the fearful barbarian invasion she'd been fighting off for so many years might even become a source of delicious pleasure. Like most late developers, she immediately set about making up for lost time; but, like all respectable girls, she had to burrow out from under a mountain of guilt and old wives' tales before she could start enjoying sex. And then she was married.

And that is where the story ends.

When the urge for procreation charged in through the front door, sexual pleasure slipped out through the back.

And now that she had been freed from marriage at long last – kicking and screaming all the way – she was frozen in a new nightmare. Just when she thought it was safe to venture into the deep end of sex again, she was frightened off by a monster that made Jaws look like a goldfish. You just can't win, as her sister Petra always said. You can't win in a world where something like Aids has become possible.

No one needed devils nowadays. Fear of Aids had created a private hell for every sinner.

This had to be the curse that the thirteenth fairy had laid on modern man. A malevolent maiden who wanted to punish mortals where it would hurt most: sex, the thing that separated earthlings from fairies.

In the last two decades before the year two thousand, this fiendish fairy had decreed, sex will become a more dangerous weapon than the spinning wheel ever was. Sleeping Beauty and everyone around her will live in anxiety, day and night, until life becomes so unbearable that no one can take comfort in sex any more. Humanity will be damned to a sleep of celibacy.

And this time Sleeping Beauty will just have to save herself. With her own hands. For what is left but hope and masturbation?

'*Masturbation, like voyeurism, paedophilia and sadism, is perverted in nature, in other words it is sexual satisfaction other than normal sexual intercourse that takes place within marriage.*' That was where everything had begun this morning, with this item in the newspaper. It had her all but choking on her coffee. It had also started a train of thought she'd tried to stop all day. Then she'd been to a party tonight and that had stoked the fire burning in her.

She stood in the crowded kitchen, a bottle of wine in one hand and a glass in the other, when her friend Anton-the-Advocate put his hands unexpectedly on her hips. She raised the bottle and the glass above her head as he pulled her against him and she laughed more in surprise than pleasure as he kissed her left ear.

'You're a very erotic woman,' he said with his mouth against her ear. 'You've got this way of brushing your fanny against the furniture when you walk through a room, as though you want to fuck the chairs and tables.'

Then he laughed too, probably at the shocked expression on her face, and asked her to dance. 'Light My Fire', Jim Morrison sang in the living room, sounding far too cool to be set alight. Luckily the music was so loud it was impossible to talk, because she didn't know what to say. '*Masculine desire is as much an offence as a compliment*', Simone de Beauvoir had said. Maybe not quite an offence, Griet thought. Heaven knew, she was grateful that there was still someone who found her desirable after her husband had so completely lost interest. But how the hell did you react when you heard something like this from a good friend – a good married friend, someone you'd never contemplated as a prospective bed-mate?

The worst of all was that Anton and Sandra were just about the only couple in her circle of friends whom she'd always regarded as happily married.

He probably only wanted to be nice, she decided. Anyone could see her self-confidence had taken a terrible knock. But the way he danced with her, his hands still on her hips, made her wonder.

She'd always found him attractive, in a boyish way, sunburnt and blond as the surfers of her schooldays. The Doors were still singing 'Light My Fire', just as they'd sung twenty years ago at school parties. Her lawyer friends alleged that a woman in the throes of divorce was the easiest prey on earth. She looked Anton straight in the eye, and then she couldn't fool herself any longer. She danced herself free of his hands. She could never again be the respectable schoolgirl who wouldn't know when the boy beside her was wanking off.

What if he'd been married to someone else, a devil whispered in her ear, someone she didn't know? Where were her grandfather's angels, she wondered, when she really needed them?

Jim Morrison had started singing something else. To burn off the worst of her libido, she danced until she was ready to drop. And to drown her spasms of guilt, she drank hopelessly too much.

And now she lay in the moonlight wishing that someone could help her through this sweaty night.

'*All this the world well knows; yet none knows well: To shun the heaven that leads men to this hell.*' Shakespeare said all there was to say about lust, Griet decided, and gave herself up to the mercy of her own hands. Shakespeare probably said all there was to say about anything.

9

Poverty and Humility Land up in Court

GRANDPA KERNEELS was a man for fishing and for peace. Not like her lawyer, decided Griet, who was too impatient ever to fish and too aggressive ever to lose an argument. But if her lawyer were like her grandfather, she consoled herself, he probably wouldn't be a good lawyer.

She sat in Hilton Dennis's impressive office and stared gloomily at the sea twenty storeys below. He was dictating a threatening letter to her husband and she wished with every word that she could turn back the Art Deco clock above his glass-topped desk. Seven years, she thought desperately, seven years ago she'd been happy.

It was unthinkable that seven years of trust and hope and love could end in an impersonal letter from a lawyer. Almost a fifth of her life, weighed and found wanting, wiped out by a cold demand for a cash settlement and some furniture. And all that remained was the echo of unbearable arguments, the bitter taste in her mouth, the blinding rage, the crippling impotence.

It would pass, she read in superficial magazine articles. The memories would fade like the view through a window that gradually collects grime. But at the moment the window was as clean as a camera lens and the memories so clear that she had to keep blinking.

*

'I can't live with you any more,' she heard George saying one night in the bedroom, his voice unnecessarily loud. She froze, toothpaste in one hand and toothbrush in the other, and stared at her reflection in the bathroom mirror. She looked old, she realized with a shock, old and tired. 'You sit up writing in the middle of the night when normal people sleep. Your word processor has become a bloody altar. Your stories have taken over the whole house.'

'When should I write if I don't write at night?' She came out of the bathroom, still holding the toothbrush, and saw that he'd started to undress. The double bed lay like a minefield between them. 'During the day I have to work to earn a salary to help you keep this house running and at the weekend I have to do the shopping and cook for the children . . .'

'Cook!' George sat down on the edge of the bed to pull his shoes off. His back was turned to her. 'One could die of starvation in this house and you wouldn't even notice. Unless you got up from your word processor by chance and tripped over the corpse.'

'Has it ever crossed your mind that you could stop moaning about what a hopeless loss I am and maybe do something around the house yourself?'

She heard a voice close to breaking and wondered whether it could be hers. He stood up and stripped off his trousers, his back still turned to her, an impenetrable shield against her anger.

'I told you long ago that you don't have to cook for me. I can look after myself, I'll eat in a restaurant, I'd starve rather than . . .'

'Rather than make a meal for me once a week?' She watched him unbutton his shirt, letting it fall to the floor near his trousers. Where his wife or the cleaner would pick it up tomorrow. She knew suddenly that she'd never hated anyone as much as she hated him right then. 'Or buy the toothpaste and toilet paper once a month? Or just once in your life put the bloody rubbish out?'

'Here we go again!' He swung round to her and she

stared at him in amazement, as though she'd never really seen him before, a skinny man in red underpants. 'Long live the kitchen revolution!'

She couldn't believe that she was married to this complete stranger. His pale eyes impersonal, his lips pressed together in a thin line through everything she said. But the vulnerability of his bony body made her heart contract, and she sank down on the bed, defeated. I love him, she thought desperately, with my whole body. And her mind had always been powerless against her body.

'I think we need marriage guidance counselling.'

'I'm sure any therapist would tell us we're mad to stay together.' George got in under the sheet and turned his back on her again. 'Anyone can see that we aren't suited to each other.'

'Because I'm a lousy housewife?'

'Because we're different,' he snapped.

'Because I write stories at night?'

'Because we want different things from life!'

'Do you know what you want from life?'

'For Christ's sake, Griet!' George sighed heavily. 'I don't know why you always pick a quarrel just before we go to bed.'

'But if we want to be together . . . if we're prepared to work at the relationship . . .'

'The question is whether we really want to be together.'

Griet took a deep breath before she could trust her voice to ask the next question.

'Do you want . . . a divorce?'

'I don't know,' George sighed, switching off his bedside light. 'All I know is that I want to go to sleep now.'

She sat staring at the frayed bristles of her toothbrush for a long time. In the silence of the bedroom the bathroom tap dripped deafeningly, but she was too old and tired to get up and turn it off.

This was the night that she was going to tell her husband that she was expecting a child of his for the third time.

*

'Are you sure you don't want any more furniture?' Hilton Dennis's question flung her back into the present. Alice who fell through a hole into Wonderland. Back to reality which was stranger than Lewis Carroll's strangest flights of fancy could be.

'No.'

Her lawyer was short and stocky, with a sparse tuft of hair that he vainly combed over his forehead, and a nose like Napoleon's. It wasn't only his nose that made one think of Napoleon, it was his whole bearing, as assertive as only a small man could be. It was this assertiveness that had earned him a good reputation as a divorce lawyer.

'I am not sure of anything any more.'

Grandpa Kerneels was a post-office clerk. From Monday to Friday he endured a white collar round his neck, but at the weekends he put on his oldest clothes and went fishing, like his father and his grandfather before him. He'd grown up in a fishing village, the waves and the legends of the sea in his blood. He'd always be a fisherman at heart.

He was a fine figure of a man with eyes as blue as the sea on a still summer's day and a dimple in his sunbrowned chin. In his young days he'd slicked his blond hair down with oil and combed it back with a middle parting. Too beautiful for a man, sighed the women in the family. Little Griet never got tired of studying his wedding picture, one of those old-fashioned portraits that the photographer had touched up by hand with a little colour here and there: Grandma Lina's lips and cheeks as pink as candy floss; Grandpa Kerneels's eyes as green as grass.

For some reason or other, the unknown photographer had decided to give him green eyes. Grandma Lina was so cross that she wanted to send the photograph back immediately. Trees are green and clouds are white, Grandma Lina believed, and her husband's eyes were blue. And there she was standing beside a stranger with grass-green eyes in her wedding picture!

But Grandpa Kerneels had an impish streak in him and

decided he liked the green-eyed portrait. Why should you go through your whole life with the same colour eyes? A change is as good as a holiday, he was fond of telling little Griet with a wink.

'I think you must also ask for the washing machine and the tumbledrier.'

'He'd never give those to me.' You don't know my husband, she wanted to say to her cocky lawyer. You don't know how stubborn he can be. 'It'll just drag the whole miserable affair out longer. And I'm tired of fighting, I'm losing my self-respect, I'm not prepared to fight over every pot and pan in the kitchen any more. I just want it all over and done with.'

'That's what they all say.' Hilton Dennis shook his head sympathetically. 'And a few months later they're crying crocodile tears because they didn't get what they should have asked for in the first place.'

'A washing machine isn't going to solve my problems,' sighed Griet, staring at the sea again. Outside, the wind was blowing wildly and the sea, whipped into white foam, looked like a massive kitchen sink. Everything reminded her of a kitchen today, she realized.

'But it'll help to keep your clothes clean,' her practical lawyer pointed out. 'And a tumbledrier can be worth its weight in gold in the wet winter months.'

'Oh, I don't know.' Griet shrugged and lit a cigarette. At least this was one place where she could still smoke without feeling guilty about her lack of self-discipline. Hilton Dennis was a chain-smoker. 'If you think it's worth the trouble . . .'

When the Second World War broke out, Grandpa Kerneels refused to enlist. Not Jan Smuts nor the Ossewabrandwag could make him change his mind. He believed in peace, he said. There were enough people who believed in war.

Sometimes you have to fight for peace, Grandma Lina said reproachfully, although she was terribly grateful that he wasn't going to leave her on her own. The war was a nightmare for everyone, but for Grandma Lina it was even worse, because she was afraid of the dark. Streetlights were turned off, car lights had to be dimmed, even house lights were hidden by hanging black paper over the windows. She would never have survived the darkness alone, Grandma Lina believed.

'My husband is better at fighting than I am,' she told Hilton Dennis, who'd switched off his little dictaphone and lit a cigarette, obviously feeling pleased with himself. He leant back in his chair a little, but without looking too relaxed. His client should realize that he couldn't devote much more time to her. The glass-topped desk stretched out endlessly in front of him, a frozen lake over which Griet had to skate clumsily. 'He confiscated my bank statements . . . He opens my personal mail and threatens me with it . . . He's accused me of stealing his video camera, and he . . .'

'This is why you came to me,' her lawyer consoled her as she heard the ice cracking around her. 'I know every trick in the book.'

'I told him I didn't know what had happened to his video camera.'

'Don't bother your head about these accusations.' Hilton Dennis played with his silver cigarette lighter, his child's hands and stubby fat-crayon fingers fidgeting impatiently. A group of legal people, she'd read without surprise in the paper this morning, had proved that they were the best liars in Britain. They'd beaten bankers, models, estate agents and clerics in the first annual competition of Perudo, a Peruvian dice game in which the competitors have to lie in order to win. 'It's all part of the game. The most important thing is not to lose patience. The one with the greatest patience is usually the one that comes out of it best.'

Easier said than done, Griet thought bitterly, if you're camping in your friend's dirty flat and you have to take crumpled clothes out of a suitcase every morning.

'In the meanwhile you should look for a better place to stay,' he suggested as though he'd read her mind.

'I can't afford a better place to stay,' she said slowly so that her lawyer would understand her. 'Not until I get back the money that I ploughed into my husband's house.'

'I'll see that you get the money back,' he said, just as slowly. 'Don't bother your pretty little head about that. Just you find somewhere to live where you can be happy.'

Hold your tongue, Griet told herself.

He stood up and came round his desk to her.

'How much longer?' she asked. 'How long do I still have to wait?'

'He gets a week's grace now to have his say,' he answered, resting a sympathetic hand on her shoulder.

'And then we apply for Rule Forty-one?'

'Rule Forty-three,' he said in a slightly patronizing tone.

'Rule Forty-three,' she echoed humbly.

Figures had never been her strong point. And her divorce was rapidly degenerating into a nightmare of figures: sums of money and important dates, how much she earned, when they'd been married, when they'd opened a joint bank account, how much they'd contributed to the house together, when she'd left the house. A year ago, Griet thought nostalgically, everything had been so simple. She'd had a house and a husband, and a baby in her womb. And neither a lawyer nor a therapist.

She got up to go to the door with Hilton Dennis. She dared not waste any more of his valuable time. Lawyers were even more expensive than therapists.

Grandpa Kerneels's ancestor was a Scottish seaman who'd secretly jumped off a sinking ship while he was expected to stand to attention and go down with the vessel. After the women and children had been loaded into the only lifeboats, he decided it was just too idiotic to stand waiting for death motionlessly. Exactly, little Griet thought the first time she heard the story.

So he leapt into the stormy sea and swam as best he

could until he lost consciousness. When he opened his eyes again, they grew wide with amazement. He'd landed in heaven, he thought ecstatically, in spite of the sinful life he'd led as a sailor. The air arching endlessly blue over him, the sand under his body as white as an angel's wings, an extravagance of green surrounding him . . .

It wasn't heaven, he was to recount later, but it was probably as close to Paradise as a sinful sailor would ever get. He'd been washed up on a pristine beach on the Southern Cape coast. The lifeboats, he heard later, had all sunk.

He became a sort of wandering teacher because, as Grandpa Kerneels was fond of stressing, he had ants in his pants. If he couldn't be on board ship, sailing to exotic destinations, he could at least be on horseback, riding over the veld to remote farms, where he taught the children his Scottish version of English and told the grown-ups the tallest of tall stories. A good storyteller, he reckoned, would always be welcome somewhere.

Grandpa Kerneels had inherited this love of stories and passed it down to his granddaughter. Little Griet had inherited it from two sides: from Grandpa Kerneels's sea stories and from Grandpa Big Petrus's angel stories. Sometimes she wondered whether she shouldn't have become a brain surgeon or a movie director instead, or gone to work in the streets of India like Mother Theresa, or done something more dramatic with her life. But in her heart of hearts she knew that she'd never had any choice.

She had to spin fairy tales to stay alive. Not just to earn her daily bread, but also to keep death at bay. Like her heroine and role model, the clever Scheherazade.

If you inherit land, you have to farm it. If you inherit stories, you have to tell them. And Griet Swart had inherited enough stories to keep herself alive for a thousand and one nights.

Riddle Tales

'We may agree, say, that contemporary
consciousness is incapable of conceiv-
ing of either angels or demons. We are
still left with the question of whether,
possibly, both angels and demons go
on existing despite this incapacity of
our contemporaries to conceive of
them.'

Peter L. Berger, *A Rumour of Angels*

10

Rapunzel Rescues Herself

'HOW ARE you getting on, Gretchen?' Gretha bent to take a roast chicken out of the oven and kept a sympathetic eye on her oldest daughter as she slowly straightened up again. She put the roasting pan on the stove and wiped a film of perspiration from her forehead with one of her bulky yellow oven gloves. 'It doesn't look as though you're getting enough to eat.'

Griet shook her head and poured her mother a whisky, just as she liked it – weak with lots of soda and a couple of blocks of ice.

'As long as you keep on cooking enough for the devil and all his henchmen every Sunday, Ma, I certainly won't starve.'

Gretha did her best to squeeze the chicken into the electrically-heated trolley with all the other dishes already keeping warm in there. She realized she wasn't going to be able to close the doors of the trolley, shrugged and hurried back to stir the mushroom sauce on the stove.

'Is it really necessary, Ma? So much trouble for one meal?'

'I know that you enjoy a proper meal now and then.' Gretha smiled and took a cautious sip of her whisky, her hand still in the yellow oven glove.

'That's not what I was asking.' Griet caught her mother's eye above the rim of the glass and Gretha looked down at the mushroom sauce quickly. 'Do you enjoy it? Standing sweating in front of the stove?'

'Oh, I don't know. "Enjoy" isn't exactly the right word. I must admit these days I'm not as keen as I used to be. Must be old age. But once I get going . . .'

If you had a mother like Grandma Lina, you couldn't help turning against kitchen chores early in your life. Gretha never played housey-housey like other little girls. She always knew it wasn't a game. She was reminded every time she was roused at night by noises from the kitchen and found her mother down on her knees, scrubbing the floor. It looked more like martyrdom than a game, and with the practical instincts of her Scottish patriarch, the one who'd jumped ship, Gretha decided she didn't want to be a martyr.

Grandma Lina's life made her daughter feel as though she were locked in a tower, but she believed there must be some way to escape. She could grow her hair, like Rapunzel, and wait patiently for a prince to come and rescue her. Or she could become a film star and marry a rich man. But Gretha was sensible enough to know she'd have to come up with another plan. To be Rapunzel you had to have long straight hair that you could throw out of the window of a tower, and Gretha's hair was as short and curly as Shirley Temple's. To be a film star you had to have the looks of Gretha's famous namesake, the goddess Garbo. Or at least be cute like Shirley Temple. And from childhood Gretha had felt clumsy and plain.

She could rely on neither a prince nor a rich man. She'd have to plan her own escape. It was a courageous decision for those days, long before Simone de Beauvoir had shaken her sisters awake all over the world.

Gretha wasn't as lucky as Sleeping Beauty, who'd had a dozen good fairies at her christening to shower her with gifts like Beauty and Wealth and Happiness. But she'd had one good fairy who'd given her one of the most precious gifts on earth. Imagination. She was a clever child who devoured books, and she decided she'd become an Authoress. If she couldn't be Alice in Wonderland, nothing could prevent her from being Lewis Carroll. Until she realized Lewis Carroll was a man.

So she just became a kindergarten teacher and told the children in her class all the stories that she'd write one day. One day, in the castle she was going to build herself, on the other side of the rainbow.

But she hadn't reckoned on love. She met a man who made her heart beat faster and her footsteps stray from the path she'd chosen. He wasn't a prince on a white stallion, just a salesman in a borrowed Morris Minor. But he was tall and dark, as she was fond of recalling. Not as handsome as Clark Gable, but so what? She wasn't exactly Vivien Leigh herself. And he certainly had the swagger of an Errol Flynn. When he drove past her house in his borrowed Morris, he'd stick an elbow nonchalantly through the open car window, supporting the roof with his right hand.

'He obviously thinks he's impressing me!' she said. Shaking her head, throughout their courtship, right up to the altar: 'You obviously think you're impressing me.' He smiled confidently and slipped the wedding ring on to her finger. He was strong, she decided, and a strong salesman was better than a weak prince.

'Remember, strength has nothing to do with muscles,' she often warned her daughters. 'Look for a man who can eat seven bags of salt with you.'

And when she wiped her eyes again, more than thirty years later, she was the middle-aged mother of five adult children. And she'd never written her stories. And she didn't know whether she still wanted to do it.

But she'd reared a daughter who wrote stories. Although no one became an Authoress these days, she thought sadly. Griet had become a writer, with a small w, as androgynous as the jeans she loved to wear.

'You grew up on old-fashioned food,' said Gretha at her stove. 'And now it looks as though you're all living on pasta and salad.'

'You brought us up properly, Ma,' sighed Griet, sitting down at the kitchen table. 'A roast and three veg every Sunday, pudding twice a week, and bedtime stories every night.'

'Nella has even become a vegetarian!'

'I'll believe that when I see her resist your venison pie, Ma.'

'Talk of the devil . . .' Her sister posed like Mae West in the doorway, a hand on one hip and an arm dramatically flung up over her head. 'How do you like my outfit, Ma?'

Gretha took a hasty sip of whisky and decided it was wiser to say nothing. Her youngest daughter, she always said, was the most wayward of the four sisters. And the other three were not exactly pillars of society.

'I heard sixties fashions were in again.' Griet wondered if she should be diplomatic. Her sister's outfit consisted of a scrap of shiny fabric above a bare midriff, long pants flaring down to the hem and the kind of platform shoes sported by classical Greek thespians. Nella worked in the Rag Trade (her emphasis) and often wore the kind of clothes ordinary people would only risk for a fancy-dress party. To hell with diplomacy, decided Griet. 'I just couldn't believe that anyone would fall for all that stuff again.'

'The sixties were an exciting time for fashion! The mini, pantihose, bell bottoms, hot pants . . .'

'Only for you people who are too young to remember the real thing,' Griet cut her sister short. 'You obviously don't have a stash of embarrassing photos of yourself in a purple wet-look outfit and laced-up boots. Or a lime-green catsuit with diamanté buttons.'

'You begged your father for that suit for weeks, Griet,' Gretha reminded her while she packed the dishwasher. 'I told you you'd regret it.'

'I remember you wearing a couple of ridiculous outfits yourself, Ma.' Griet smiled at her mother who was crouching wearily in front of the dishwasher. She'd never let her hair grow. It was still short and curly. 'Do you remember the photo Pa took that day at the zoo, Nella?'

'Who could ever forget it? It's the sort of photo you discuss with your shrink years later. It's the sort of photo that lands you up with a shrink in the first place!'

Nella poured herself a glass of soda water and sat on the kitchen table, swinging her legs.

'Ma in a shocking-pink Crimplene mini in front of a hippo that looks as though it's going to charge her any minute.'

'I hope your daughters take the mickey out of you one day too,' Gretha laughed, holding her back as she straightened up. 'If you ever get around to –'

She was suddenly busy about the stove again.

'Ma,' Griet said with a sigh. 'The fact that I haven't managed to bear a c-h-i-l-d doesn't mean that you have to feel guilty every time the word slips out.'

'Oh, Gretchen, I do worry about you so.'

Griet looked at her mother and shook her head. Gretha's lovely face had become one mass of wrinkles the last few years. It was only her hair – the same shiny brown it had been in her girlhood, without a hint of grey – that held invincible age at bay.

'You always make out that everything's fine, but I know how badly you want a baby ... And now, with George leaving ...'

There was nothing like a mother's concern to bring a lump to your throat, thought Griet.

'It's true,' agreed her sister. 'You're always so busy being the efficient big sister, you're actually a pain in the arse. Why don't you just relax for once? Tell us you're having a hard time. Or do you think we'll reject you because you can't cope?'

Almost eight weeks without a man, she'd written this morning in her Creative Arts Diary. And she missed his sons almost more than him. She wondered how they were getting on at school, where they were going to spend the holidays, which TV programmes they were watching on Friday nights these days.

She'd seen them in a shopping centre the week before,

75

two laughing blond boys with gangly arms and legs. They'd walked past quite close to her without seeing her, two children she'd fed every weekend for seven years: Michael, the serious first-born, and Raphael, his devil-may-care sibling. She'd watched them develop, she thought bleakly, from chubby-cheeked toddlers into rowdy school-boys and now these almost adolescent strangers.

She had to restrain herself from calling out their names, from running after them. They were chips off the old block, she could see quite clearly, with their father's bony shoulders and loose-jointed arms. She was the outsider. She faced the fact finally. Goldilocks in the bears' house.

'It's terrible to be a stepmother. You're the villain of every fairy tale. And if your husband throws you out, you lose all claim to his children. As though they were bits of furniture that belonged to him. I miss Michael and Raphael and I can't see them. I'm having a hard time.'

'See? You said it and you're still sitting here,' Nella cried. 'You weren't struck by lightning.'

'But it's not as bad as it was a month ago,' said Griet, jumping up to go and set the dining-room table. 'I was ready to put my head in the oven then.'

Her mother and sister laughed nervously as she left the kitchen.

'Don't worry, Ma,' she heard Nella's voice behind her. 'She's only joking. She's not the suicidal type.'

If her sister only knew what her shrink knew.

On the way here this morning she'd listened to a radio report about a man who'd gassed himself in his car. He'd stuck a notice on the windscreen: *Beware! I have Aids! Wear gloves!* The police had praised his action, announced the newscaster, deadpan. Griet nearly drove into the car in front of her.

Somewhere in a police station, she fantasized, a circular letter is being drawn up right now: *'To protect the safety of the community, the following groups of people must be encouraged to commit suicide: ANC activists, PAC terrorists, Communists and Atheists, End Conscription Campaigners, Any Other Agita-*

tors, Et cetera, Et cetera . . .' And right at the bottom of the list: '*Aids Sufferers.*'

It's dangerous to travel alone, she thought, and it's getting worse all the time.

She walked into her brother who'd just appeared in the front door, his long hair windblown from his motorbike ride and his cheeks as pink as a sleeping child's. Marko was the baby of the family, the boy who, according to his father, was reared for the devil: spoilt to hell by an angelic mother and four older sisters. Griet tended to agree with her father. But he was the only brother she'd ever have.

'Mirror, mirror on the wall, who is the fairest of them all?' teased Marko with the words she'd taught him as a toddler.

'You, O King, are handsome,' smiled Griet, 'but your oldest sister, who lives with the seven dwarfs over the mountains, is a thousand times fairer than you.'

'I'm so hungry I could eat a whole sheep.'

He threw an arm round her shoulders and went back to the kitchen with her.

'I thought you weren't eating mammals any more,' Nella accused him, jumping down from the table.

'Hell, you look more like a clown than ever.'

'Community service, my brother.' Even with her platform shoes she fitted in under his arm. Marko was tall and thin like Grandma Hannie's people, with Grandpa Big Petrus's gigantic hands and feet. 'Don't you think we need clowns these days?'

'Sure. Clowns and fairy tales. Between you and Griet maybe you can still save the country.' He kissed his mother on the cheek. 'With your food, Ma, to feed the starving masses.'

Gretha wiped the lock of hair from his eyes, radiant because three of her children were together under her roof. But Griet knew she was wondering what the other two were eating today, wherever they were in the world. A mother never really gave up her children, she knew even if they'd only lived in her womb.

'And why are your eyes so big, Ma?'

'All the better to see you, my child.'

'You're all mad.' Nella got her brother a beer from the fridge. 'My boyfriend says it sounds as though my whole family believes in fairy tales.'

'There aren't many other things to believe in,' said Marko.

'What's wrong?' Gretha asked quickly.

'Nothing.' He took a few thirsty gulps from the beer bottle. 'The army's looking for me again. I'm thinking of going to live in Namibia, now that they're becoming independent.'

'It's not so bad, Ma,' Griet said comfortingly when she saw the expression on her mother's face. 'Namibia is much closer than the Netherlands. You can go and visit him there'.

Marko had completed his military service a few years earlier without undue question or crisis of conscience, like most white boys who'd just written matric. Two years later, considerably older and wiser, he returned to reality and became a press photographer. He was convinced that he could never serve in the defence force again.

But he also didn't see his way clear to sign declarations and go to jail. He'd just keep on the move, he decided. If they couldn't track him down, they wouldn't be able to call him up for further military camps. It's the easier way, he said in bitter self-mockery, for chaps who don't want to be martyrs. He also probably took after his patriarch who'd bailed out of a no-win situation.

Griet had often wondered what her grandfather would have done if he'd been born a few decades later – Grandpa Kerneels who'd believed in peace because there were enough people who believed in war. Would he have gone to jail rather than shoot at township children? Would he have chosen voluntary exile in Europe rather than military service?

No, she thought, Grandpa Kerneels would probably have chosen to keep on the move too. Hers wasn't a tribe of martyrs and heroes.

'Where's Pa?' asked Marko, to change the subject.

'Can't you hear the thunder of the gods?' giggled Nella, hopping back on to the table. 'He's building again.'

'Another room?' he asked in surprise.

'No,' said Gretha sheepishly. 'Help me get this trolley into the dining room. He's changing your old bedroom into a bar.'

'A *bar*?'

'A man must have a bar, he says. Somewhere his wife and children can't bug him. A room of his own.'

'And where do the wife and children go if they want to get away from him?' Marko asked as he pushed the trolley out of the kitchen.

'Pa must watch out,' said Griet, following her mother and Marko, guilty because she hadn't laid the table yet. 'He's behaving more and more like Grandma Hannie's mad brother. Before you know it, he'll have built himself a tower in the back yard.'

'Your father's been mad for ages,' said Gretha calmly. 'But in a different way to Grandma Hannie's people. He'd never sit in a tower waiting to die. He'd get a franchise to supply coal to the devil. He'd make sure that he was so indispensable that he'll never be removed from earth.'

She must get herself tested for Aids, thought Griet as she laid the table. It was the right thing to do. It was brave and admirable and responsible. Like standing on the deck of a sinking ship while a sinking band played 'God Save the Queen'.

But what would you do if you heard you were an Aids carrier? Bringer of bad tidings? Messenger of the gods?

The unbearable burden of a carrier.

If you heard you had cancer you could still find escape in the little death. In the moments before an orgasm you live with every nerve, with every muscle and every organ of your body – animal and irrational. Maybe the big death was also like that, maybe in the last months you learnt once more to value the animal side of life, of hunger and thirst, pain and relief, sex and sleep.

But someone with Aids loses even the final wordless comfort that two bodies can offer one another.

Griet polished a knife absent-mindedly on a corner of her mother's starched tablecloth. She wasn't brave enough, she knew that. She didn't come from a brave family.

The Children of Eve Learn to Laugh Again

'JANS IS torturing himself again,' said Griet's friend Gwen at an exhibition opening. 'He's not supposed to drink beer because the workers are on strike. But the beer's on the house here. What's the poor man supposed to do?'

Jans stood in a corner of the packed hall, beer in hand and a drawn expression on his face – as though he hoped no one would notice him if he didn't move. For a change he wasn't wearing a suit or tie but he still looked as though he were standing before a magistrate in court, as uncomfortable as it was possible to look in jeans. Griet and Gwen sat on the floor looking at the people who were looking at the works of art on the walls.

'Luckily I don't like beer.' Griet smiled and raised her wine glass to attract Jans's attention. 'So I don't have to suffer with him.'

'Do you know how badly the workers on wine farms are paid?' asked Gwen seriously, waving at someone she recognized. 'And they can't even strike: they don't have a union. Just imagine how the farmers would shit themselves if they had to pay fair wages.'

'So I shouldn't really drink wine either,' sighed Griet.

What's left, she wondered gloomily, to make life worth while? Cigarettes give you lung cancer, marijuana makes you stupid, coffee brings on heart attacks, chocolate makes you fat, sunshine causes skin cancer, alcohol hammers your liver, money spells sleepless nights, make-up enrages the feminists, pregnancy leaves you with stretch marks, politics lead to despair and sex gives you Aids. She really couldn't blame her children for refusing to be born.

'No, you can drink as much as you like,' Gwen told her, 'as long as you seem guilty about it. Just look at Jans, he's perfected the technique. Enjoying himself thoroughly, but making it look like every moment is sheer torture.'

'I wonder if the artists here know anything about the beer boycott.' Most of the people around them were young and white, wearing T-shirts with cartoons or political slogans, and staring at the paintings as though they'd discover the meaning of life in them if they only had sufficient patience. Griet and Gwen had been invited to the opening by a friend who created 'significant sculptures', according to a *Cape Style* reporter who obviously hadn't known what else to say about his work. 'Maybe they're so busy Creating Art that they don't have time to read the papers. Maybe it's only political lawyers like Jans who take the Struggle seriously.'

'I don't know about you, but I'm just about Struggled out. Just look at all the crap on the walls here. Everything is so "relevant" I could puke.'

'And so desperately serious,' sighed Griet.

'The whole world is in an uproar because the whale is endangered. Stuff the whale, I say. We should spare a thought for the Happy South African instead – also in danger of extinction.'

Griet burst out laughing at her friend's vehemence. Gwen, sitting cross-legged beside her, had broad hips and a rounded bosom but her haircut was so short and masculine it almost distracted attention from her abundant body. Like most women, she'd have preferred a different one.

'After the Grahamstown arts festival last year I was so exhausted by the breast-beating I had to spend a week in bed,' said Gwen glumly. 'If I'd had to endure one more relevant painting or play, I'd definitely have cut my throat. In the end I spent a whole evening watching TV sitcoms just to make sure my laughing muscles still worked.'

Griet folded her arms round her knees and examined her Levi jeans with some concern. She'd heard the other day that the indigo they used to dye denim could cause skin cancer if you didn't wash your jeans in boiling water. And these days she didn't even have a decent stove to boil water, let alone a washing machine. If she got skin cancer, she thought with grim satisfaction, it would be her husband's fault.

'When did you last read a funny Afrikaans book?' asked Gwen sombrely.

'Well, I found the latest Ena Murray omnibus quite absurd,' said Griet with her chin on her knees.

'I mean apart from Jan Spies and all those guys with funny accents. I'm talking about a Funny Afrikaans Novel. Was there ever such a thing as a Funny Afrikaans Novel?'

'I'm sure someone must have written a thesis about it.' Griet smiled unwillingly at the deadly seriousness with which Gwen discussed humour. 'What about Etienne Leroux?'

'One clown with sunglasses doesn't make a circus, Griet. I am talking about a whole tradition of humour: irony, satire, absurdity, fantasy. We imitate everything the Americans do, why can't we also learn to laugh as we read? Give the devil his due, just think of Salinger and Heller and Irving and Updike and Vonnegut . . .'

'Well, we do have Herman Charles Bosman,' said Griet. 'But he didn't write in Afrikaans.'

'OK, South African, then, Afrikaans or English. But not something that was written fifty years ago. What about the last ten years, what about "this moment in time" as the politicians like to put it?'

'Tom Sharpe?' Griet suggested apologetically.

'He doesn't count.' Gwen was relentless. 'He had to go and live in England before he could joke about South Africa.'

In his corner, Jans hunched his broad shoulders and tensed his neck muscles as though he were about to charge through the crowd to the nearest door. He looked more like a rugby forward than ever, Griet thought, amused. Ill at ease in a room full of art. It was only the beer that kept him here.

Hugging her knees closer, Griet frowned. Her left breast felt tender in this position. She lifted her chin a little and tried to touch the breast unobtrusively. If she got breast cancer, it would also be her husband's fault. Her own hands would never be as familiar with her body as his were. Since he no longer touched her, it was only her gynaecologist who stood between her and her worst nightmare.

But these days she had so many fears that even breast cancer had lost some of its old horror. To die alone had to be worse than going through life with one breast.

> My husband is snoring in the bedroom [her friend wrote from England], and the alcohol fumes from his open mouth are strong enough to kill flies. I wish I could patent him and send him to Africa. Talk about killing two flies with one blow.

It couldn't be as bad as it sounds, Griet comforted herself. Louise wasn't the type to become a martyr. Not even for a foreign passport. And she'd always believed that a decent dollop of exaggeration could only make a good story better.

'Where's Klaus tonight?' Griet asked Gwen because she didn't want to talk about the seriousness of Afrikaans literature any more, especially with someone who refused to laugh about it.

'At marriage guidance,' said Gwen so bitterly that Griet's eyes darted to her face. 'With his ex-wife.'

'What for?'

'You may well ask.' Gwen sat with her elbows on her knees and her chin in her hands. 'Their son's apparently psychologically disturbed. Not that one could blame the poor kid – with a father and a mother as different as Capitalism and Communism. Just think what an identity crisis you'd have if your mother were Dolly Parton and your father Fidel Castro.'

'Marilyn Monroe married Arthur Miller.'

'And look what happened to Marilyn Monroe.'

'So they've decided to go to marriage guidance?'

'To dig up the old skeletons and make sure they can't be brought to life again.'

'I thought marriage guidance was for marriage . . .'

'They call it relationship counselling these days,' explained Gwen, 'because no one wants to get married anymore'.

Klaus didn't want to get married again, Gwen always said, because his divorce had been so messy. And she didn't mind, she insisted staunchly, because she wasn't sure she wanted to take such a radical step. In the meanwhile they'd lived together like a married couple for years.

'How do you feel about it?' asked Griet carefully, sounding unexpectedly like her shrink.

'I've never felt so threatened in all my life.' Gwen ran a distressed hand through her short hair. 'No, I lie, I have. When I was in Standard Five and I had to go to a new school and no one wanted to be friends with me.'

'But Gwen, it's unthinkable that Klaus and his ex-wife would . . .'

'Almost as unthinkable as it was a month ago that the Berlin Wall could be broken down overnight?' Gwen smiled ruefully. 'Have you seen the last *Time*? "*Berliners embrace in unbelieving joy*" is the headline on the cover story.'

An East Berliner, Griet had read in the paper this week, brought back two library books which he'd borrowed in West Berlin on 9 August 1961. 'I couldn't exactly throw the books over the Wall,' was the grey-beard's apology. The books were Thomas Mann's *Death in Venice* and F. W. Foerster's *The Jewish Question*. The library had apparently let him off the fine which amounted to more than five thousand rand.

'Maybe they deserve each other, God knows they're both emotional cripples.' Gwen began to laugh at herself. 'I know! I'm bitter because he never wanted to go to a shrink with me. I mean, it isn't as though we never had our own problems. I want a child and he doesn't want another one, and some time or another we're going to have to do something about that. And now he's in therapy with his former wife because of their son. Does that mean his son is more important to him than his relationship with me?'

Griet shook her head because she didn't know what to say. Her own impending divorce seemed to have opened the floodgates of her friends' unhappy secrets. She wondered if she still knew anyone who could live happily ever after with someone else.

I chucked orange juice at my husband last week [wrote Louise from London]. It was in the living room. I had a glass of juice in one hand and a knife in the other, and I opted for the juice. I still feel proud of my self control. Then he chucked coffee at me. Luckily he wasn't holding anything else, because he'd most likely have chosen the more lethal weapon. I think men do it automatically. Once they lose control, they lose it completely.

And now I'm battling to scrub the orange stains off the landlord's white sofa. I don't know what the Brits put into their orange juice, but it must be a kind of dye. I never thought I'd miss a washing powder, but I miss Omo!

PS: Do you still have so many men killing their own families?

Anton and Sandra, she thought sadly – she'd always been so sure of them. They'd started going out as students. Anton became an average advocate and Sandra was an average mother of two schoolchildren, and they were crazy about each other and their children and the big house where they were sure to live happily ever after.

But since she'd felt Anton's hands on her hips, she wasn't so sure any more. Maybe she was wrong, maybe her own lust made her unnecessarily suspicious. Maybe for ever after is just too long, too much to ask. Maybe one should only aim at a year or three.

'Divorced men have unbelievably complex relationships with their children.' She tried to dredge some consolation from her own limited experience. 'It has to do with feelings of guilt and uncertainty and defensiveness and God knows what else.'

'I don't know,' said Gwen, leaning her head back against the wall and closing her eyes. 'I don't know whether it's worth the trouble any more.'

Jans looked round him, his eyes glazed above his round spectacles. Griet raised her glass again to attract his attention. This time he noticed and, smiling with relief, pushed his spectacles back up the bridge of his nose.

'"*Some thirty thousand gods on earth we find, subjects of Zeus and guardians of mankind*",' he said as he collapsed on to the floor beside them. 'That's according to Hesiod. And yet you can't call on a single one to protect you against art exhibition openings.'

'Or marriage therapy,' smiled Griet.

'Or relationships,' said Gwen, opening her eyes again.

Who's Beauty and Where's the Beast?

GRIET WAS taking off her dressing-gown, one leg already in bed, when there was a knock at the door. She cast a startled glance at her alarm clock. Midnight!

Tidings of death, she thought, tying up her white gown again and hurrying to the door. She wondered what would be worse: to find someone with the news of a death in the family; or to find no one – and to wonder if perhaps she'd follow in Grandma Lina's footsteps three nights hence.

Her hand was shaking so badly it was difficult to unlock the door. The Angel Gabriel smiled at her through the bars of the security gate, a golden halo round his head and a white robe on his body. Griet went weak at the knees.

'Am I at the right address?' asked the stranger in a soft, husky voice.

'No,' said Griet anxiously, looking for the sickle in his hand. No! That was crazy! Gabriel was the one who brought good news. 'I mean, I don't know. Who are you looking for?'

'Griet.' *'Greetings, most favoured one!'* He spoke with an English accent, she realized. An angelic accent. 'Griet who is living in Louise's flat.'

'That's me.' It was the streetlight shining on the back of his head that gave the illusion of a radiant halo, she realized with a twinge of disappointment. And the white robe was actually a loose shirt and what looked like a piece of cloth wrapped round his loins. But she was still nervous, until she saw the dust on his bare feet. There couldn't be dust in heaven, she decided. Not with Grandma Lina up there. 'Who are you?'

'Adam.' And he was truly as beautiful as the first man must have been. Young, Griet thought, terribly young. Now that she could see him properly she decided he looked more like a surfer than an angel. 'Louise said I could come and stay.'

'But I'm staying here!' Griet protested, overcome with anxiety again.

'But didn't she write to you?' He shook his head in confusion. 'Hey, never! I don't believe it. She said you wouldn't mind if I stayed with you for a few days.'

'But there's no space in this flat!'

How could her friend do this to her? she thought desperately. Legally, she was still a married woman. Admittedly a married woman who'd forgotten how even to spell sex ages ago, but nevertheless a married woman. And now this young image of an angel who called himself Adam was standing at her door – though still on the other side of the security gate – asking if he could sleep with her. She took a deep breath.

'There's only one bed,' she said determinedly, 'and I can't share it with you.'

'Sure!' Adam burst out laughing, quite deflating Griet. It just went to show, as Grandpa Kerneels would have said, you can't always add one and one and be sure of getting two. With her sort of luck the man was probably gay too. 'But isn't there, like, a couch or something? Or I could sleep on the floor: I've got a roll-up mattress down in the car.'

'But I can't just let you in, I don't know you, I don't even know if you . . .'

'*Lead us not into temptation, but deliver us from evil.*' What if the man were a psychopath or a con artist? Maybe he didn't even know Louise.

'This is getting really embarrassing,' the stranger said.

Suddenly she felt Adam's sublime eyes on her breasts and realized she was wearing nothing under her dressing-gown. The guilty way his eyes shied off convinced her that at least he wasn't gay. If he raped her now, she thought even more desperately, he would testify in court that she'd led him on.

'Look, I'm sorry. It's like . . . Louise said she'd write to you.'

> My husband says we should go for marriage therapy [Louise had written to her], but I don't know if anything can save our relationship. On the other hand, we can't carry on chucking coffee and wine and tea at each other; the whole flat is covered with stains. If this is married bliss, Griet, then count me out. I thought it might be easier the second time around, people are supposed to grow up, but I've never behaved so idiotically in my life.

But she hadn't written anything about Adam.

'Hey, I tell you what,' suggested Adam from behind the bars, 'why don't you ring her?'

'In the middle of the night?'

'It's not that late in London yet.' The man was beginning to sound desperate too. His soft voice sounded even huskier. He might be even younger than her brother. 'I'll pay for the call. Just ask her if she knows me. Or are you going to leave me standing out here all night?'

Griet cursed her friend, not for the first time in their acquaintance.

'I'll ring her from the office tomorrow,' she decided, and unlocked the security door. Now she was certain that she was going mad. But sometimes a woman has to trust her intuition, and hers told her that this man was harmless, in spite of his strange appearance. 'You can sleep on the sofa.'

'Thanks,' he said with a sigh of relief. 'I'll nip down and get my things from the car.'

He was wearing a sarong, she saw as he walked away, and his mane of hair was fastened into a loose ponytail at the nape of his neck. Imagine what her father would say about a man who wore a dress! But she'd married a man any father would have trusted. She'd spent seven years with a man who was the epitome of respectability in his tweed jacket, grey wool socks and old-fashioned round-toed shoes. She'd been driven from her house by a careful man with a respectable job and enough life insurance to support five wives. And here she was hiding away from life in a dirty flat full of cockroaches. No, Griet decided, she wasn't going to be as fearful as Grandma Lina.

13

Simple Gretchen Dreams She's Clever

'*I DON'T WANT* to come every week any more,' said Griet. Rhonda's eyes widened a fraction. 'I only want to come twice a month.'

Griet felt she'd scored a victory. Could she at last have said something that surprised her shrink?

'I'm glad to hear that,' said Rhonda. She didn't sound glad. 'As long as you remember that I'm always here when you need me.'

'Thanks.' Though it wasn't true. She couldn't ring Rhonda when she really needed her. Between midnight and first light, when all Grandma Lina's fears came back to taunt her granddaughter, when anxiety weighed on her chest like a ton of bricks – that was when she needed her shrink. Then, when Rhonda was sleeping peacefully beside her rich husband in her two-storey house, her children safe in their rooms full of toys, the whole nuclear family protected by an alarm system, two watch dogs and a high garden wall. *Help me, Rhonda, help me, help me.* 'I'll ring you if I can't cope.'

'How are you getting on with the divorce?'

'We aren't getting on, we're going backwards.' Griet was struggling against the suction power of the chair that she was rapidly sinking into. Today she wanted to be dignified, to show Rhonda that she could get by without her, even if only temporarily. 'We've got to the stage where I'm being accused of theft and fraud. With general delinquency as an alternative.'

'And it'll get worse before it gets better. I know it isn't much comfort, Griet, but it's only what happens in the majority of divorces. The one who's hurt worst is usually the one who slings most mud.'

'Are you trying to tell me George is still capable of any feelings?'

'It isn't easy to acknowledge how badly someone else can hurt you,' said Rhonda in her most sympathetic voice. 'It's much easier to stay angry the whole time.'

'Not the whole time any more,' she objected quickly. 'I don't think about him all day any more.'

'But you dream about him at night?'

Griet stared at Rhonda in amazement. So this is what had become of all the witches in the world – now that they flew in Boeings instead of on broomsticks. This was how they made a living these days. They hadn't lost their mystic powers. They'd become psychotherapists.

'It usually happens when you begin to control your thoughts consciously,' explained Rhonda. 'That's when the unconscious takes over. You can't control your dreams.'

Three nights ago she'd dreamt that George was knocking at her door. He was naked except for a strategically placed fig leaf. Wings sprouted from his back. He was smiling as she'd last seen him smile before their wedding. He had the video camera she was accused of stealing and he raised it up to film her. She wanted to invite him in but her security gate had a series of locks and all she had to open it with was a huge icing-sugar key – the kind you get on a birthday cake when you turn twenty-one. The harder she tried to release the locks, the faster the key crumbled. By the time she got to the last lock, the key was reduced to a few crumbs of icing sugar. Her body was wet with perspiration when she woke up.

'That's a good sign,' was Rhonda's consolation when she saw Griet's face. 'You have to digest your emotions consciously and unconsciously. It takes time, but you're on the right track.'

'*Divorced men spend more time in hospital than married men, they have a shorter life expectancy and are twice as likely to die of cirrhosis of the liver*', Griet had read in the paper that morning. She'd thought about the dirty glasses in her husband's sink and underlined *cirrhosis of the liver* so determinedly that she tore the newspaper.

After that she'd turned to the boring property pages and continued her half-hearted search for somewhere to live.

'But what becomes of all the years you loved someone?' Griet was wearing red today, the same colour as Rhonda's sofa. She always reached for the red in her wardrobe when she was feeling greyer than usual. She'd never seen Rhonda in red. 'Or do you simply have to accept that everything is going to be buried under the mud during your divorce?'

'As long as you remember that in the long run mud bakes dry and flakes off. In a few years you might even be able to be friends.'

'And sprout wings and gently soar up to heaven?'

'Griet . . .'

'Of course.'

Rhonda wore creamy white and other peaceful shades – pale blue like her eyes, a peachy colour like her lips. Even witches were no longer what they used to be. Who sang that song about being so tired of living and so afraid of dying? Certainly not the Beach Boys.

The night before last she'd dreamt that she had something very important to say to her husband, but she could only communicate with him through a children's game. Everyone stood in a long line and the first one whispered a message to the second one, who whispered it to the third one, and so on, until the last one heard a hopelessly garbled version of the original message. There were any number of people in the line, from junior-school friends whom she'd last seen twenty years ago to the sunburnt surfer who'd ridden her virginity like a wave. 'THIS IS YOUR LIFE!' someone yelled excitedly. It took so long for the message to get to George that she almost woke up. A lifetime later he stood up, scarcely visible at the far end of the line, cupped his hands round his mouth and shouted: 'Brziffgtprkss! She woke with wet cheeks. Did children still play Chinese whispers?

'But in the meantime I have a more immediate problem,' she admitted while she peered at Mickey Mouse on the wall. 'There's a man in my flat. Someone Louise got to know overseas . . .'

'And?'

'He's terribly beautiful . . . and terribly young.'

'And . . .'

'Not very clever.'

'What does that mean?'

It meant that she wanted to fuck the man all night long, Griet thought rebelliously. With clothes on, without clothes on, on the bed, on the balcony, on the stove, in the oven, on top of Table Mountain, Devil's Peak and Lion's Head, and in the cable car, swaying between heaven and earth. Why did you always have to spell everything out to your therapist?

It was on days like this that she wished she was more like her rag trade sister. Nella didn't agonize for weeks about whether she wanted to sleep with someone or not and whether it would be worth the trouble and how the hell she was going to feel about it for the rest of her life. She certainly didn't discuss it with a therapist. She listened to her body.

'Do you know a man called Adam?' Griet had asked Louise in London the morning after the stranger had knocked at her door.

'Shit,' mumbled Louise, still half asleep. 'I forgot to warn you.'

'Against what?' Griet's voice sounded shrill in her own ears. 'Warn me against what?'

'That he'd probably pitch up there.' Louise had dropped the receiver on to the floor with a clatter and picked it up again with some difficulty. 'But I didn't think he would.'

'Well, it's too late to warn me against anything, because right now he's alone in your flat – stealing the taps and the doors for all I know – and I didn't sleep a wink all night because I didn't know whether he was going to rape me or murder me –'

Louise roared with laughter and Griet broke off her sentence in confusion.

'Relax, Griet, relax! I got to know the guy here in London and he wanted to go to Cape Town and I suggested he stayed there with you. I think he's just what the doctor ordered to help you shake off those divorce blues.'

'Are you out of your bloody mind?' Griet's voice had risen with her unease again. 'How well do you know him? Where the hell did he get a ridiculous name like Adam?'

'Where the hell did you get a ridiculous name like Griet?'

'Ask my mother!' Griet shouted. 'I always wished she'd called me Snow White.'

'Well, there are people who have to struggle through life with a name like Adam.' Louise giggled, and laughter started to tickle Griet's throat too – a frog that would leap out if she opened her mouth. 'I mean, there's Adam Ant and Adam . . .'

'. . . and Eve?'

'I thought you'd be grateful if I sent you a nice man!' laughed Louise. 'You're always complaining that they've become collectors' items in Cape Town.'

'How do you know he's a nice man?'

'How do you ever know?'

Griet could literally hear Louise shrugging.

'Where's his family?'

'Shit, you sound like an old woman. What does it matter?'

'I feel like an old woman. He looks about twenty. And he wears a dress.'

'His family is somewhere in the Eastern Cape, Griet,' Louise said in the patient tone people use when they're speaking to toddlers and the mentally disabled. 'He came here five years ago because he didn't want to fight for the

South African army. He got a British passport because his grandfather was born here. He wanted to be with his family for Christmas. And I don't know how old he is but he's older than twenty.'

'What about his underpants?' Griet giggled.

'Let me know as soon as you find out.'

'I read in the paper that General Noriega of Panama has a passion for red underpants. Did you know that? And I always laughed at my sister when she said it was a dictator's colour.'

'Well, let that be a lesson to you.'

Griet sighed.

'Listen, Miss Prissy,' said her friend, 'if you didn't think he was nice, you'd never have let him into the flat.'

'How's it going with the marriage therapy?' asked Griet.

'Shit. The arsehole is misusing it to try and floor me with his accusations. It's incredible: he keeps bringing up things I'm supposed to have done wrong two years ago. Things he's never said anything about before. Can you believe that men can nurse grievances like this?'

'Well, he probably feels safer with the therapist than he does when he's alone at home with you. Shame, he's been soused in orange juice so often . . .' Griet was giggling again. 'He probably smells of citrus fruit by now. There's a man in every flavour?'

'My best friend,' Louise sighed.

'OK, I know what you're talking about,' Griet consoled her. 'My own experience of marriage therapy was traumatic. In the end we had worse fights in front of the therapist than we had at home. The only difference was the presence of a referee.'

'How long did you stick it out?'

'Only a couple of sessions. Then the ref chose my side. That's how George saw it, anyway. He refused to go back.'

And she was still stuck with Rhonda, who couldn't do anything to save her marriage, and apparently could do just as little to help her through her divorce. Witches could cast spells, she thought. Witches in their offices. Here she was sitting in a witch's office with a witch who could cast spells. But one couldn't expect miracles.

The fact that she couldn't even choose her own therapist surely summed up her life with George. When her husband finally agreed to marriage therapy, at the insistence of their GP rather than the insistence of his wife, he chose the therapist himself. It didn't matter to Griet, she was only too thankful that they were going to be able to discuss their problems with someone. But when Rhonda told George one day that he was wasting his money, he looked at her like Jesus must have looked at Judas after that kiss.

'I can't help you if you refuse to be helped,' Rhonda said with the closest approximation of emotion that Griet had ever seen her display. George could even make his therapist sound old and tired. 'You can't help an alcoholic who refuses to admit that he is an alcoholic.'

George shook his head. He'd thought his therapist would be an exception. But in the end, like all women, she wasn't clever enough to understand him.

'So what!' Griet let off steam to her sister Tienie. 'So what if he is cleverer than his shrink! Sometimes I think even *I*'m cleverer than my shrink.'

After that afternoon she knew that it was no longer worth the trouble of fighting with her husband. Their therapist had condemned their marriage to death. All that remained was a few weeks of waiting in a house that had become a death cell. Waiting for the end and hoping for a miracle, *deus ex machina*, fairy godmother, angel from heaven, reprieve from the state president. And in the end there wasn't even a Last Supper. The executioner had come to fetch her unexpectedly in the middle of the night, not shortly before sunrise as it happens in books and movies.

'Do you remember Robertson Davies's *The Rebel Angels*?' her clever sister asked. 'Do you remember the advice the decadent priest gave the young girl? Stay out of the hands of a shrink who is less intelligent than you are, even if it means you have to bear your misery alone.'

'But I am also more intelligent than my mechanic and my plumber, Tienie, and it doesn't mean that I can fix my broken car or my dripping tap myself. It's possible that you can be cleverer than most therapists, but that they can help you nevertheless. They're trained, just as a mechanic is trained to open the bonnet of a car and fix the engine. They're trained to open you up and dig about in your emotions. Anyway, that decadent priest committed suicide in the end. Or am I thinking of another chap who wanted to bear his misery alone?'

'Isn't that perhaps what the writer was trying to say?' asked her clever sister.

Last night she'd dreamt she stood before a stove wearing red high-heeled shoes and yellow oven gloves, cooking for her husband and an unknown guest. But an insatiable hunger gnawed at her stomach and she ate everything as fast as she took it out of the oven: crisp roasted chicken and golden potatoes, crunchy on the outside, and sweet potatoes and honeyed carrots gleaming like dark orange flames on the tongue, and cauliflower under an eiderdown of cheese sauce, asparagus that melted in the mouth, broccoli *al dente*, beetroot staining the rest of the food red . . . And still she was hungry, hungry, hungry. When her husband got home, she was too frightened to tell him not a morsel of food remained.

She asked him to sharpen the carving knife and she opened the door to the unknown guest – Anton in one of his wife's dresses – and yelled: 'Listen, he's sharpening his knife, he thinks we're having an affair, run for your life!' And when Anton ran away, she yelled at George: 'Run, he's eaten all your food and stolen your video camera! Catch him!' And when George took up the carving knife and charged after Anton in his wife's dress, she took off everything except the yellow oven gloves and caressed her body . . . and woke up with wet loins.

*

'That means,' she told her therapist, 'that I can't look a winged horse in the mouth.'

That meant that she wanted to tell her therapist to go to hell.

Sometimes one needs swear words. Strong words, magic words, spells. *Brziffgtprkss!*

14

The Black Sisters

GRIET'S SISTER Tienie had inherited her mother's hair and her father's temper. Everyone in the family said so. Short Shirley Temple curls and a shorter than short temper. But right now she was sitting at a restaurant table, radiantly happy, with no trace of the seven devils she sometimes carried around with her.

'Let me guess,' said Griet opposite her. 'You're in love.'

'A holiday romance.' Tienie nodded. 'It probably won't last. But it doesn't matter. I'm old enough not to think this is for keeps every time I meet someone. Not any more.'

'I'm glad to hear it,' said Griet as it behove an older sister to do. 'Who's the lucky lover?'

'Someone local.' Tienie smiled mysteriously. 'With a gorgeous beach house up the West Coast.'

'So that's where you're going to hide these holidays.'

Griet took in her sister's curly hair and unmade-up face: she still looked like the teenager that she'd been years ago. 'I suffer from a small man complex,' Tienie had said herself. 'I can't impress my students with my stature. I have to vanquish them with my brilliant brain and fearless tongue.' And when she frowned, her abundant eyebrows met over her nose making her look fearsomely bedevilled.

She'd always been more independent than her sisters. She was the only one who'd ventured out to an English-medium university. Now she worked as a sociology lecturer – at an English university in Johannesburg.

'Have you seen Ma and Pa?'

'I'm having supper with them tonight.'

'Alone?'

'Me, myself, I,' she hummed over the rim of her tea cup.

'Without the lover?'

'Anything to keep the peace.' Tienie shrugged, pushing the sugar bowl round the table. 'I've already given them enough shocks.'

'I don't think anything that you or Nella pitch up with at home could still shock them. Do you remember the time Nella invited a boyfriend with a wooden leg and an eye-patch over for supper?'

'The one Pa called "Shiver Me Timbers"?'

'Ma thought the eye-patch was a new fashion and asked him if he wouldn't be more comfortable if he pushed it up while he ate. So he obliged and it turned out he didn't have an eye under it. Ma tried so hard not to look shocked!'

A young waitress was hovering near them, her blue-shadowed eyes fixed on the moving sugar bowl. It was a smart restaurant and an expensive sugar bowl and they both looked out of place here, Griet realized. Tienie was dressed in her holiday clothes – floral shorts and a striped T-shirt and trainers without laces – and Griet wore one of her familiar crumpled dresses, the uniform she chose for hiding in her office.

'Petra also brought a few weirdos home before she became the world's leading yuppy.'

'Do I hear she's coming out for a visit?' asked Tienie.

'Just after Christmas. For more than a month. Ma is on cloud nine.'

'Without hubby?' Tienie raised her heavy eyebrows expressively.

'Hubby has to stay behind in the Big Apple to keep the home fires burning.'

'And to keep his wife in designer clothes.'

Tienie and Petra didn't burn with enthusiasm for each

other, Gretha always said, and they certainly weren't warmed by the same fire. Of course not, said Tienie, the nearest Petra ever came to any fire was the flame on her elegant silver cigarette lighter. Tienie regarded Petra as a capitalistic *femme fatale* with an irrelevant, superficial job in the advertising industry. Petra regarded her sister Tienie as a socialist feminist who talked a lot of crap.

'That's one black sheep that turned snow white.' Griet smiled with her chin in her hand. 'These days Pa regards her as the most exemplary of all his children.'

'Well, she's the only one who's making any money. Maybe that's all that counts for him.'

It was because they were such opposites, Gretha always said, that Tienie and her father could never get on. No, said Tienie, it was because she'd dared to be a third daughter rather than the son he'd wanted so badly. She'd always shone in the classroom and on the sports field, but he'd just shaken his head and said she was too competitive for a girl. She'd have a hard time finding a husband.

'And the only one who's decently married,' said Griet. 'Since my fiasco.'

'How are you coping?' Tienie leant closer in concern. Now she played the older sister. 'I mean, I know how one feels when a relationship breaks up . . . but how do you cope when a baby dies?'

'You don't cope.' Griet stared at the cup in her hands as though she could read the future in it. The porcelain was so thin it was almost transparent. The restaurant had better crockery than she'd ever had at home. 'If I smash this cup against the wall, I could maybe stick it together again, but there'll be bits that I can't find. That's probably what happens every time someone you love dies . . . your mother or your husband or your brother . . . If it's your child, there are so many bits missing there's not much left to stick together.'

But on a certain level a failed relationship is worse, thought Griet. Death makes you feel powerless, but a divorce makes you feel guilty. You have no control over death, but you have to accept responsibility for a divorce.

It was the guilt that was torturing her; the guilt and the responsibility.

Sometimes she wondered whether her inability to bear a child was also her fault. Whether she was being punished because she preferred writing to cooking. Preferred sex to ironing.

What if she had to choose? Between bringing up children and writing stories?

Her throat closed and she couldn't get a word out.

'As far as the relationship goes . . .' she said gruffly at last. 'I'll probably always wonder if I didn't give up hope too easily; whether I couldn't have done more to save it.'

'Such as?'

'Not locking the keys in the car.'

When she was discharged from hospital shortly after the birth and death of her baby, she and George had got to the car before she realized she'd left her flowers beside her bed. They were the only flowers she'd received – a bunch of creamy-white roses her husband had brought her, white-knuckled. She asked him to go back and fetch them. He sighed, put her case into the car and went back into the hospital building.

She got into the car, feeling more alone than she'd ever felt in her life. It was so unbearable that she got out again to run after him. When they returned to the car, the keys were locked inside. George didn't say anything, just bit his lip, picked up a brick and took out all his frustration on the window. It was the only time she ever saw him lose control.

'I can't decide whether I did too many things wrong,' she tried to explain to her frowning sister, 'or just didn't do enough things right.'

'What do you think you did wrong?'

'You sound just like my shrink. One always does something wrong. Let he who is without sin throw the first stone.'

'And you sound just like Grandpa Big Petrus, always quoting from the Bible. Except that he knew the proper words.'

'You cope from day to day.' Griet poured herself a third cup of tea. It was quite cold by this time. The waitress was still watching them with anxious eyes. She seemed to be scared they'd make off with the china. 'But not always from night to night.'

'I know. When I lie awake in the dark, I think: This is what hell must be like. Very dark and very alone.'

'I'm not brave enough to lie in the dark.' Griet took a sip of tea and grimaced – it tasted worse than she'd expected. 'I'm worse than Grandma Lina was. I turn on every light in the flat before I go to bed. Last week was a bit better, with Adam in the living room. Just to hear someone else breathing . . .'

'Tell me more about him.' Tienie leant forward again.

Griet wondered what the two women at the table next to them were talking about. They were much more smartly dressed than the two Swart sisters, in suits with high-heeled shoes, but their heads were just as close together.

'I don't know very much. He knocked on my door in the middle of the night. He's tall with brawny shoulders and a golden body. I was probably mad to let him in, but I felt sorry for him.'

'"*Be kind to strangers, for some who have done this have entertained angels without realizing it.*"'

'Where did you get that from?' Griet asked, delighted.

'Guess! It begins with a B.'

'Impossible!'

'"*Don't forget about those in jail. Suffer with them as though you were there yourself.*"'

'One of Jans's friends has a bumper sticker that says that.'

'It's well known in the Struggle. Hebrews 13, verse 3. But verse 2 is much more beautiful: "*Don't forget to be kind to strangers . . .*"'

'Entertaining angels without realizing it . . .' Griet repeated slowly. 'Well, so far I haven't seen an awful lot of this angel. I'm in the office and he's on the loose. But he says he wants to make a meal for me this weekend. To thank me for letting him stay. I'm only too pleased that someone wants to use the oven for something other than suicide.'

'Do you mean . . .'

'No, I don't mean anything.'

Tienie shook her head incredulously.

'You mean he can cook?'

'Seems like it,' Griet smiled and dropped her chin into her hand again. 'He apparently worked in a restaurant sometime or another.'

'You've finally met a man who can look after himself!'

'Now I must just find one who can look after me as well.'

'You can look after yourself.'

'I know, I know, I know, I'm not talking about physical care,' she protested to her indignant sister. 'But it would be nice to find someone who doesn't run away when the "for worse" in the "for better or for worse" happens, you know, Tienie.'

'I never know what he wants!' said the woman at the next table, suddenly animated. 'I just never know what he wants!'

Griet started to laugh, nearly choking on the dregs of cold tea in her cup.

'You have to keep on guessing, my dear,' comforted her elegant friend, painting her lips a bloody red while she peered into a little hand-mirror.

'Now you sound like Ma again,' giggled Tienie. 'Look for a partner who'll eat seven bags of salt with you. Wasn't that what she always said?'

'That's what she still says.' Griet gestured to the waitress with the starched lashes to bring their bill. 'Strength has nothing to do with muscles. Just look at your father.'

'That's why I'm gay.' Tienie looked at the young waitress and then at the two old friends at the next table and shook her head as though there were something she couldn't understand. 'Because Ma taught me that strength doesn't lie in muscles. I just don't know if Ma is ever going to accept that she had anything to do with it.'

'Cover yourself, my darling sister,' said Griet, her voice faltering unexpectedly, 'so the rain doesn't fall too hard on you, so the wind does not blow too cold on you ... Do you remember?'

'So the king may see how beautiful you are ...' Tienie said absently.

15

Cinderella Loses Her Glass Slipper
(*Et Cetera, Et Cetera*)

MAYBE HE hadn't read Camus, but she couldn't really say he was stupid. You don't learn everything out of books, either, she'd realized again last night.

Griet lay on her stomach, looking at the sleeping form beside her. He was naked, shameless as a child, the sheet flung aside. She'd never manage to look as relaxed with nothing on. Especially not with the blue veins on her legs or the pads of flesh on her hips clearly visible to a stranger's eyes in the bright morning light.

Not that there was any detail of the honey-brown body beside her that should be kept hidden under the sheets. It was probably as close to a perfect body as any she'd ever get into her bed. Not even a hint of fat or flab. Not one single pimple on the buttock. Even his penis looked as though it had been dipped in honey, shiny after a night of sex, the same healthy colour as his shoulders.

She normally felt disconcerted waking beside a naked man whose family she didn't know. She was probably old-fashioned, but she preferred having her body discovered little by little, from forehead to foot, from top to bottom. Certainly not the other way round. It was just that every-thing had happened so quickly last night that she'd lost control of the sequence. Adam had slipped her sandals off and started massaging her feet . . . Next thing she knew, here she was lying as naked as Eve before the serpent led her astray. And it didn't even occur to her to cover herself with the sheet.

Adam had cooked dinner on the gas stove and they'd sat on the floor eating it: a meal that had far exceeded her naughtiest dreams. Fresh artichokes to start with, then a seafood paella, and then the *crème de la crème* of desserts: cunnilingus on the dusty living-room floor, under the merciless light of a bare bulb, with the South African national anthem on TV as background music.

'We won't be able to say tomorrow that we were seduced by the romantic atmosphere,' Griet warned, shutting her eyes against the blinding light. 'We won't have any excuse.'

'Hey, man, we don't need an excuse,' mumbled Adam, his mouth against the curve of her instep. 'Romance is for people who feel guilty about sex.'

Griet was speechless. The boy wasn't as innocent as he looked, she thought as his tongue slid over her ankle and his hands stroked up her legs, right up to the thighs and then back to the ankles. She felt like an insect pinned down by an angel, squirming on the floor as her skirt worked its way up higher and higher. How on earth had she landed in such a divine position? She'd been eating, her desires reasonably under control, when she realized he was staring at her foot. He'd slipped off her sandal without a word and taken her foot in both hands. Her fork had clattered to her plate.

'I don't know about you,' she said, swallowing hard, 'but I have reasons to feel guilty about sex.'

'*Thou shalt not commit adultery*,' someone who looked like Grandpa Big Petrus exclaimed from the top of a mountain, and the earth beneath her trembled. Or maybe it was only a thrill of pleasure.

Adam raised his head – his mouth set on a steady course for her thigh – and flashed her his Angel Gabriel smile.

'You're the kind of person who has to feel guilty before you can enjoy anything.'

Once again his insight – and what his mouth and his hands were doing to her thighs – took her breath away. The lower body as dessert, she'd thought while she could still think. Just the other day a friend had told her about a new sex handbook for women by an American with long blonde hair and long red nails, photo on the back cover slightly out of focus, age unspecified. She advised her readers to sample their own sexual juices.

You wouldn't put a plate of food in front of your husband if you weren't prepared to taste it yourself, would you? Not only did you taste different from other women, the book claimed, but your taste also varied on different days of the month. As a good sex partner you should know when your good days are – vaginal-gastronomically speaking – and when you shouldn't open the restaurant Mount Venus.

Griet wondered whether she shouldn't have taken the American writer's advice, but Adam thrust his head between her thighs with the eagerness of an animal about to slake its thirst. The sharp light against the ceiling and the numbness in her wide-splayed legs reminded her momentarily of the maternity ward, but that was her last coherent thought of the night. After that everything happened without giving her a chance to think. Without a clear boundary between agony and ecstasy. Like in a maternity ward.

After thousands of years of philosophy and logic, thought Griet in her bed beside a man she barely knew, Western civilization was still virtually powerless against man's animal urges. Intellect still had very little influence on birth, sex and death, the three greatest experiences in anyone's life. Thank goodness, thought Griet, raising herself on an elbow to admire Adam's hair, which was fanned out long and loose on the pillow beside her.

There were ways of making sex less bestial, she reminded herself. Ministers, priests and other clerics were often experts in this field. And clever men who were afraid of losing control.

When she and George had first had sex they'd whispered so as not to wake his children. And like so many things that are done early in a relationship without any thought for the consequences, the silence in their bed had almost immediately become a web in which they'd spun themselves fast. Even without children in the vicinity, George's accompanying noises were limited to a few approving groans or dignified grunts. He believed that sex, like women, was better seen and not heard. If you held your tongue in the heat of battle, you wouldn't let anything slip out that could be used against you later. You wouldn't say something as rash as *I love you*.

And as they normally only found time at weekends once the boys were in bed, there wasn't much to see either. George would switch off the light and reach for her. It was a silent, dark affair.

Sometimes the violence of an orgasm forced her mouth open, but time and time again the shriek froze in her throat. She felt like that poor screaming woman in Munch's painting, trapped in silence for ever after.

But last night, on the living-room floor, she'd shrieked. Last night she'd taken vengeance for every woman who'd ever been gagged by a man. For Munch's poor model and for all the women who were burnt or drowned because they were suspected of witchcraft, and for all her fairy-tale heroines who weren't able to save themselves, and for all the stepmothers who always got the lousy roles to play, and for seven years of decent, civilized, *silent* sex.

And Adam snorted and cavorted along with her, MGM's roaring lion, her fingers tangled in his mane of hair, her legs locked high over his jerking back, her teeth in his neck, a dragon spewing fire from his loins, a devil skewering her on his trident and leaping over the moon with her, an enchanter whose tongue licked away all resistance. Anything but an angel.

Maybe it only happens once in a lifetime that precisely the right sexual partner comes knocking at your door at precisely the right moment. '*Angel visits*', said the dictionary that she kept at her bedside. '*Delightful intercourse of short duration and rare occurrence.*'

Once upon a time there was an angel and a witch, but sometimes the angel was wicked and sometimes the witch was good, and in the end no one knew which was which, not even the witch and the angel themselves. But an angel would be silent during sex, thought Griet. So George must be an angel. The thought made her shake with laughter.

Adam stirred and reached out indolently, without even opening his eyes. He touched her back gently, feeling his way downwards, blindly, and sighed happily when his hand found her buttock. He lay motionless for a few moments and she wondered disappointedly whether he'd dropped off to sleep again. Then he started to caress her thigh slowly. The memories of last night were enough to open up the floodgates of sensation again.

'*Angel n. Divine messenger;* (*fig.*) *loving or obliging person.*' She'd been given over to the mercy of this hand, sliding down the inside of her leg. '*Witch n. Woman supposed to have dealings with devil or evil spirits;* (*fig.*) *fascinating or bewitching woman.*' Which of the celestial teams would she choose to fly for? The angels with their wings were so terribly serious; like the English; like Louise's husband who wouldn't even pass wind in front of anyone else. But the witches on their broomsticks could be just as humourless; like the White Left in her fairy land. The angels with the seriousness of religion, the witches with the humourlessness of politics, and Griet Swart with an identity crisis.

'How's the guilt?' asked Adam in a croaky, early morning voice. His eyes were still closed.

'What guilt?'

He opened his eyes and turned his head slowly to her.

'Hey, are you OK?'

'I can't remember when I last felt this good.'

'When did you last have sex?'

'Long ago,' sighed Griet, 'Long, long ago.'

Witches obviously had better reasons than angels to be Angry Young Women. It was hard to laugh when you were standing on a pyre. In the three centuries after Pope Innocent VIII had published his infamous *Summis Desiderantes* in 1484, almost nine million witches were systematically executed in the name of the Father, the Son and the Holy Ghost. And it wasn't over yet, thought Griet, her throat contracting. In the terrible country where her own fairy tales were set, women were still burnt as witches, stoned, stabbed to death.

'No wonder you jumped on me like a wild animal,' said Adam, pulling her on top of him, his eyes closed again.

'I did not jump on you! I was eating my supper and the next moment I was flat on the floor! I couldn't even protest because my mouth was full of calamares.'

'It's the way you eat that drove me berserk. I figured anyone who enjoys food so much must also be into sex. Even if she feels guilty about it.'

'I'm telling you, I don't feel guilty any more.'

'Hey! This sounds like sin!' He pulled her head against his neck and ruffled her hair into an even wilder mess. 'We can't have you living without guilt. We'll have to do something about this.'

'I can't think of anything we've left undone.'

'Where's your imagination?' sighed Adam with his mouth in her hair. 'I thought you wrote fairy tales?'

'Exactly,' answered Griet. 'The princesses in my fairy tales would never get laid on a dusty living-room floor.'

'Imagine what they're missing,' whispered Adam in her ear.

'Can I ask you something?'

'Anything.'

'Do you always keep a condom handy?' She felt the laughter well up in the body under her cheek. 'Or did you know what was going to happen last night?'

'Hope springs eternal.'

Griet rubbed her face enthusiastically against the hair on his chest.

'*Two women aged sixteen and seventy-one years were burnt to death at Izingolweni.*' She drew her fingers through his pubic hair and felt him grow hard. '*The following day a fifty-year-old woman was struck with a stone and then set alight in Oshabeni.*' She'd always been amazed at how easily a man could get an erection in the morning. '*A woman was burnt to death and another woman killed with a sharp instrument in Enkulu.*' It was like witchcraft: abracadabra, you take hold of him and part of his body changes before your eyes. '*On the same day at Msinbini a forty-year-old woman was set alight.*' In the last years of her marriage it had been the only power she still held over her husband. '*At Maguchana a sixty-year-old woman and a thirty-year-old woman were burnt to death.*' Sexual sorcery in bed in the morning – until he'd started sleeping in another bed.

'*The police said all those killed were suspected of witchcraft.*'

16

Whatever Happened to Rumpelstiltskin?

THE CHRISTMAS tree was small enough to stand on the coffee table. Nella had decorated it in gold and silver: it was as stylish as the grown-ups' trees you see every year in glossy magazines.

Griet would have preferred a naïvely kitsch tree, with flickering lights and shaving-foam snow and all the other over-the-top decorations children love. She crouched before the tree in her parents' living room and touched the spiky foliage. Even an artificial tree decorated by a child would have looked more alive than this real one turned into a piece of pretentious artwork.

A year ago she'd looked forward so much to this Christmas Eve. She had been seven months pregnant and irrepressibly excited about the adventure that lay ahead. She must be patient, her analyst told her: memories were like blood that congealed to form scabs. The problem was that dates kept coming up that scratched the scabs off. Tonight everything was all bloody again.

A year ago she and her husband had been alone, his children with their mother, her parents holidaying at the coast. She wanted to be with her parents, but he wasn't in the mood for a family Christmas. So she'd given in and spent Christmas with her silent husband in his silent house.

*

'Next Christmas everything will be different again,' she promised him over a glass of sparkling wine. 'The baby might even be crawling by then.'

They sat alone at the long dining-room table in the empty house. It was impossible to believe that anything between them could ever be different to this unbearable reality. But she wanted to believe it so badly.

'The house won't be so quiet. Michael and Raphael will be here. I want to get a proper Christmas tree, and a turkey and plum pudding and all the trimmings, and invite my family over to join us for a change, for a real –'

'Is it necessary to involve your family in the extravaganza too?'

'Christmas is supposed to be a family feast.' She laughed nervously because she didn't want to quarrel on Christmas Eve. There were enough arguments, there were enough other evenings. 'We could also invite your family, I don't mind, but you probably wouldn't . . .'

'I can't wait.' George studied the trout on his plate critically. The fish looked raw, Griet realized. It was the first time she'd cooked trout. 'It sounds like the perfect evening. My AWB brother will no doubt fall for your lesbian sister.'

'George, I know it's boring of me to be fond of my family.' She felt as though she were posing for a camera, the muscles round her mouth sore from smiling. 'I'd like to be able to suffer with you because I don't get on with my parents and my siblings. It might have given me something to write about.'

'Are you sure this fish is cooked through?'

'Trout is supposed to be pink.'

She tasted the fish cautiously. It wasn't raw. She was so relieved that she drained her glass in one gulp.

'If I could have chosen, I would perhaps have chosen different parents. I don't know, but I couldn't choose so I have to try to make the best of what I got. But it could definitely have been worse, it could have –'

'I don't have a quarrel with you and your family, Griet. Just leave me in peace, that's all I ask.'

He spat out a mouthful of bones. Naturally he'd divided the fish so he got more bones than flesh in his mouth. George dragged a sack full of thorns with him through life, regularly strewing them over his own path.

'It's the only family I'll ever have,' she murmured.

Had she married a frigid man, she asked herself, or had their relationship frozen his emotions? Had there been any warmth long ago? Or was it just her fertile imagination that made her mistake a freezer for an oven?

Why had she grown so chilly after seven years with him that she wanted to climb into an oven?

'I don't even like my own children all the time.' His mouth was unexpectedly vulnerable, without the normal mocking smile; there was no trace of cynicism in his eyes. 'Can't you understand that I'm depressed about the arrival of another one, Griet?'

She put out a hand and touched his cheek. She'd always been defenceless against his vulnerability. I love you, my husband, she thought. As God is my witness, I love you.

'It's too late to do anything about it now,' she said, folding her other hand protectively around her belly.

She shouldn't have tempted fate.

She'd given her husband a jersey for Christmas, a cable-stitch sweater that she'd spent weeks knitting in secret. It was thick and the wool made her hands sweat and she kept wishing she was lying under an umbrella on a sunny beach. Once upon a time, long ago, there was a girl who was ordered by a king to spin gold from straw, otherwise she'd be put to death. A dwarf had appeared to help the poor girl with his spells, but he'd demanded an impossibly high price. She had to promise to give her first-born child to him.

Never knit a man a jersey before you're married, her mother had always told her, it's unlucky. Griet had laughed at her superstitious mother. Anyway, she was married. She felt safe.

In the end she had to give up her child even though she hadn't had a dwarf to help her with the knitting, even though her husband never once wore the jersey.

It wasn't the first time she'd given him something he didn't like. Her only comfort was that he hadn't done much better himself. It was as though they were unconsciously competing over who could give whom the most unsuitable gift.

She'd given him a white cotton dressing-gown that he'd never worn, and he'd given her a crocheted tablecloth she'd never used. She should have known that he'd rather wrap a towel around himself than wear a dressing-gown and he should have known that she hated crocheted things. She frequently gave him books that he never read: gardening books a week before his interest in gardening evaporated like the early morning dew on the lawn; carpentry books just after he'd sold all his tools without telling her; philosophy books by writers he regarded as intellectually inferior. He gave her perfume that made her smell like a prostitute, cookery books with the sort of recipes a dyslexic child could follow, and a green and yellow Swatch that didn't go with anything in her wardrobe.

Maybe he was trying to encourage her to get Springbok colours for some sport or another, Louise had suggested.

'Wear it with a black beret and a clenched fist to one of Jans's parties,' Gwen suggested. 'It'll do wonders for your credibility in the Struggle.'

After seven years they seemed to be bound together for ever by an unbreakable chain of inappropriate presents.

'And why are you sitting here all on your own?' asked her father behind her. She swung round guiltily. 'Or are you trying to escape the racket in the kitchen?'

'I should go and help them,' she said, jumping up from the Christmas tree, but her father stopped her with a raised hand.

'You don't have to, they're just talking, your mother and your sisters.'

Hannes sat down on the sofa as carefully as an old man. His hair was quite white, she noticed with a surprise. In his young days, he'd been tall and lean like his son, but the last few years he seemed to have grown steadily shorter and smaller, like a balloon that's leaking air.

She felt slightly ill at ease, as she always did when she was alone with him. She could never understand that a salesman should have so little to say to his children. To sell something, you have to be able to communicate with your customers, don't you?

No, Griet corrected herself, he has plenty to say to his children, sometimes even too much, and he says it regularly. He liked launching into long monologues at table, usually with a glass of wine in one hand. He would have made a good preacher or Shakespearian actor, if he knew the Bible or *Hamlet* half as well as he knew his precious literature on sales techniques. *How to Sell Absolutely Anything to Absolutely Anybody*, Tienie called everything her father read. With the subtitle *Death of a Salesman's Family*.

'You must believe in yourself,' Hannes always said. 'You must be positive and have faith in yourself, then you can do anything you set your mind to. It's easy to be negative. Easy and cowardly. If you tell yourself you can't do something, you're protecting yourself from the risk of failure. To be a spectacular success, you have to be willing to be a spectacular failure. Nothing ventured, nothing lost, but nothing gained either.'

His family had grown accustomed to his monologues over the years, learnt to listen patiently or laugh tolerantly, even tease a little sometimes.

But no one could ever accuse him of communicating with his children.

He liked to hold forth about positive thinking and how to get rich and which rugby teams were going to make it to the Currie Cup final. It was a pity that none of his daughters was particularly interested in who would win the Currie Cup, but, after all, what could you expect from women? His son's lack of enthusiasm was harder to accept, but then his mother had spoilt him rotten from the day he was born.

Sometimes he also talked about politics and religion. 'The problem with black people is that they're too different from us,' Hannes always said.

'The problem with children is that they're too different from parents,' sighed Nella behind his back.

'Coloureds aren't a problem – they share our language, religion and habits – but the blacks just aren't as highly developed as we are. You can't simply hand the country over to them. Look at what's happening in the rest of Africa. The whites are pulling out and economies are collapsing, the streets are littered, the schools are deteriorating and the public services falling apart.'

'Sounds like Britain,' Griet would interject when she wanted to be provocative, 'after ten years under Thatcher.'

But she usually preferred to hold her tongue.

'The public services can't really get much worse than they are already,' said Tienie, who always found it hardest to keep quiet. 'When were you last in a post office, Pa? Or a provincial hospital?'

That normally started a fight.

But if you asked him about his emotions, he was the one who went quiet. The ease with which he talked about positive thinking was matched only by his embarrassment if you expected him to say something about fear, uncertainty or love. The idea that there were people who would consult a therapist of their own free will gave him gooseflesh. Griet never discussed her shrink with her father. It was even a bit of a battle talking to her shrink about her father.

'I hate Christmas,' Griet sighed, sitting down beside him on the sofa. 'I never liked it – I mean since I stopped believing in Santa Claus – but I've never hated it as much as I do this year.'

He didn't meet her eyes; just nodded sympathetically.

'It was one of the biggest disappointments in my life when I heard that Santa Claus was my own father in my mother's dressing-gown.'

'You always believed in that kind of thing more easily than the other children,' Hannes said thoughtfully. 'Santa Claus and the Easter Bunny and the Tooth Mouse.'

'I still have an extraordinary capacity for self-deception.' Her father cast a surprised glance her way. 'But when I first started doubting Santa Claus ... It was like pulling a cornerstone out of a wall. The whole wall collapsed.'

Hannes had grown up the hard way – he said so himself. There'd always been enough food in Grandma Hannie's labourer's cottage – bread and butter, eggs and meat. But there was never enough money for luxuries like school shoes or sports clothes. And fantasy was a luxury. Grandpa Big Petrus had his angels, but that wasn't fantasy, they were as real as religion. And, unlike the Easter Bunny and the Tooth Mouse, the angels didn't cost anything.

'I only heard about Santa Claus when I went to school,' Hannes had told Griet years earlier. 'I thought he must have lost my address, otherwise he wouldn't have overlooked me all those years. Then I decided to write to him explaining in detail how to get to our place, and just mentioning in passing that I wanted a rugby ball or a bike. Who knows, maybe he'd make up for all the years he'd missed me?'

Hannes wrote to Santa Claus, but said nothing to his parents. Grandpa Big Petrus, he knew, was too proud to accept anything from a stranger in a red outfit. On Christmas Eve he hung up his pillow-case in the living room beside the sofa on which no one but the *dominee* ever sat. If it was good enough for a clergyman, it would be good enough for Santa Claus.

Hannes was a middle child, like his difficult daughter Tienie. If he'd received a present from Santa Claus that night, he'd have felt more special than his brothers and sisters for the first time in his life. He was so excited that – also for the first time – he battled to fall asleep.

Of course the pillow-case was still empty next morning.

'I stopped believing in Santa Claus there and then.' That was how he always ended the story. 'I never believed in anyone but myself again.'

'Are you happy, Pa?' Griet asked him on the sofa.

'Tonight?'

'No, I mean generally. You're always so positive, you're actually a pain in the butt. Like Nella tells me I am,' she added quickly. 'You're always busy with some project or other — changing a bedroom into a study or breaking a new window through the living-room wall . . .'

'You have to keep busy,' he answered exactly as she'd expected he would, 'otherwise you start asking too many questions.'

'What's wrong with too many questions?'

'You've asked too many questions since you were a little girl. The devil finds work for idle fingers.'

'And you think in the end I'll be seduced by the devil?'

'I wouldn't say that.' He smiled. 'But if you don't get answers, you could get negative and depressed. And before you can say Jack Robinson, you'll find yourself wondering whether anything is worth the trouble any more.'

She'd already reached that stage, she wanted to tell her father, but she didn't know how to. Her father thought it was terrible to ask too many questions. She knew it was worse to get too many answers.

'Do you know the story about the young man who came across Death at the roadside, Pa?'

Hannes raised his eyebrows and shook his head. The skin of his neck was starting to sag, Griet noticed. He was beginning to look like Grandpa Big Petrus had looked years ago. Why did an old person's skin stretch like a jersey that had been washed too often? When did the air start leaking from the balloon?

'Well, Death was lying at the roadside and the young man helped him to his feet, and Death was so grateful that he promised to send a messenger before he came to fetch him. So he could get ready. The years went by and the young man became an old man, but he always comforted himself with the thought that Death would not come upon him unannounced. And then one day Death tapped him on the shoulder and said he'd come to fetch him.'

Hannes stared at the Christmas tree on the coffee table, his hands folded over his paunch, his face relaxed.

'"But you told me you'd send a messenger!" cried the old man, sorely put out. "I sent one messenger after another," said Death. "I sent sickness to lay you low and toothache to plague you. I sent age and wrinkles to warn you. And every night of your life I sent my silent brother, Sleep, to remind you of me."'

Hannes nodded slowly, his eyes still fixed on the Christmas tree.

'Don't you sometimes feel unhappy because you wanted more from life, Pa?'

He was silent for a few moments before answering thoughtfully, 'I would really have liked to own a Mercedes Sport.'

He was probably serious, Griet realized in dismay.

'I'll pour us some wine,' he said, getting up. So that she couldn't pry any more, thought Griet. 'Red or white?'

'White, please, *Pappa*.'

'It'll be better next Christmas,' he mumbled almost inaudibly as he left the room.

'Next Christmas everything will be different,' she said to herself once she was alone.

17

The Five Fellow Travellers

ONCE UPON a time, long long ago, there lived a wicked stepmother, Griet wrote as she lay in her bed, her heart longing for George and her hormones lusting after Adam. Once upon a time there was a stepmother who was thrown out of the castle by the king. No, no, no, she thought. This is no good. I'm going to seek my brother and my sisters and together we'll teach the king a lesson.

The stepmother didn't have many talents, but there was one thing she could do better than anyone else. She could blow: there was a superhuman power in her cheeks and her mouth; her lungs were like hot-air balloons. (She didn't smoke, obviously.) She could blow because since childhood she'd had to blow life into stories, day after day, month after month, year after year. By the time she was thirty she could blow the Cape Doctor's tablecloth of cloud right off Table Mountain, blow the smoke from the Devil's Pipe into the sea, blow away the mist that hung around Lion's Head. All the better to see you, my child. She could blow the Twelve Apostles' hair awry.

Enough is enough, Griet decided in her bed. *She could blow*, she added for good measure, inscribed a triumphant exclamation mark and turned the page.

The blowing stepmother rushed furiously through the

world, searching for her sisters and brother. In a city between the devil and the deep blue sea, she found her youngest sister with a hat perched over one ear. 'You look like a clown!' she said. 'Why don't you put your hat on properly?'

'If I put it on properly,' answered the clown, 'it immediately gets so cold that the angels in heaven freeze and fall to earth like statues.'

'Come with me,' said the blower. 'Together we're going to teach the king a lesson.'

'Where's the new man in your life?' asked Nella the moment she stepped into the flat. 'I'm eaten up with curiosity.'

'He's not the new man in my life,' said Griet, leading her sister to the kitchen.

'The new man in your bed?' Nella stopped short and put her nose in the air. 'Isn't this a bit over the top, Griet? Only old hippies still burn incense.'

'Well, I had to find something that smelt stronger than insecticide.'

Maybe she'd overdone it a bit, she realized, with joss sticks wherever you looked. Even one in the oven.

'I gather you're still battling with the cockroaches.'

'*A luta continua*. But it's not only cockroaches now. The past week millions of ants have also signed up with the Struggle. I swear they're going to carry me off in my sleep.'

Nella examined the kitchen critically while Griet examined her sister's outfit just as critically. Nella was wearing a satin waistcoat over a transparent chiffon blouse – nothing under the blouse – and very short shorts on her long brown legs. The sort of outfit that would count against you in a rape case, Griet thought worriedly. But it was probably only mothers and older sisters who were haunted by these fears. She poured Nella a glass of almost frozen white wine.

'Sorry, the fridge is a bit dicey. I should have taken the wine out earlier.'

'At least you still have a fridge.' Nella shrugged.

'Not that it's worth much. Every second day it doesn't work at all. The rest of the time it freezes everything from wine to tomatoes as hard as rock. It's one of the reasons I've never invited anyone to come and visit me.'

'I'm beginning to understand why you're so relieved to have found another place to stay at last.' Nella laughed, following Griet out of the kitchen. 'How did you stick it out here so long?'

'I didn't really have any choice.' Griet had over-decorated the living room with flowers to disguise the lack of furniture, but now, as she stood in the middle of the room viewing the place through her stylish sister's eyes, she knew that her diversionary tactic hadn't worked. 'It's beyond me how Louise could choose to live here.'

I want to move out [Louise wrote from London], but there are so few places here that I could even sort of afford that it's maybe less trouble to stay married. I know you'll think I'm copping out, but what the fuck, you're the one who wants to believe in fairy tales. Maybe most marriages are as unsatisfactory as ours, maybe most people prefer to stay unhappily married rather than being single. The therapist looks bored to tears with everything I say. As though he hears exactly the same story every day. That's what makes me wonder.

I wish I could find an Afrikaans therapist. It's hell having to worry about your tenses while you're trying to pour your heart out.

Meanwhile my husband is drinking more and more and saying less and less. I've heard this one before somewhere. One evening after our therapy session he suggested we get some fish and chips and have sex for a change. Not in exactly the same sentence, but in the same tone of voice. There are very few things in our relationship that still amuse me, but that struck me as so ridiculous I laughed until I cried.

'So where's the mystery man?' Nella persisted.

'He's gone to his family for Christmas,' Griet explained, trying to wash away her impatience with a swig of wine. 'He's on his way back now – hopefully he'll pitch up in time to come to a New Year's Eve party with me.'

'But I'll be gone by then.'

'I don't know why you're so keen to meet him. It's not as though he's going to be your brother-in-law or anything. I mean, I've slept with the man a couple of times, that's all. And he's going back to London in a week's time.'

'We're all worried about you,' said Nella, disappointed. 'It's time you met a solid man.'

'I don't think "solid" is the first word that'll come to Pa's mind if he sees Adam's ponytail,' Griet said with a smile.

'What do you think of him?' Nella asked Tienie when she arrived a few minutes later.

'He's terribly good-looking,' said Tienie, sitting down on the floor. 'And that's an objective assessment, if you take my sexual preferences into account.'

'I never thought I'd ever sleep with such a beautiful man again.' As Griet went to the kitchen to fetch a beer for Tienie, she added, more to herself than her sisters, 'I was beginning to wonder whether I'd ever sleep with any man again.'

'I was also beginning to wonder,' Nella called out after her. 'You waited long enough before you made a move.'

The clown and the blower journeyed on together, Griet fantasized before the open fridge, until they reached a city where everything was made of gold. Streets, buildings, mountains, even people. There they found the third sister who was so strong that she could carry off all the stunted trees in hell with one hand behind her back.

'Come with us,' said the blower. 'Together the three of us will teach the king a lesson.'

The three journeyed through the world and over the water until they reached a city where dreams come true, and there the fourth sister awaited them, her bag already packed. 'I knew you were coming to fetch me.' She had such good eyesight she knew the colour of the man in the moon's eyes. 'I saw you before you came over the water. Together the four of us will teach the king a lesson.'

And together the four journeyed back over the water until they reached a deep dark forest, where they found their brother who was standing on one leg with his other leg lying on the ground beside him.

'What's happened to you?' they asked in surprise.

'If I use both legs,' answered the brother, 'I run faster than a witch can fly.'

'Come with us,' said the blowing stepmother. 'Together the five of us will teach the king a lesson.'

'My self-image is in tatters,' said Griet, back in the living room. 'I look in the mirror and all I see is that I am seven years older, that I have seven times as many wrinkles and flabby muscles. I can't believe any man will ever find me attractive again.'

'That's fucking sad.' Tienie's eyebrows formed a thick black line under her words. 'And just because one man doesn't want you any more.'

'It isn't necessary to emphasize "man", Tienie. Don't you feel the same when a relationship fails?'

'My self-image has never been attached to smooth skin and taut muscles.' Tienie tipped her glass slightly and poured the beer with a deft movement of her wrist. 'That's what's sad, Griet: that someone like you suddenly sounds like an ageing beauty queen.'

'I know my life isn't dependent on my appearance.' Griet took a quick sip of wine. 'But it's important to men, whether we want to admit it or not. It's a fact like the sun rising in the west.'

'The east.'

'Wherever,' sighed Griet. 'Sure, there are other ways to

attract a man's attention. I mean, I could fling myself off my balcony and hope that a guy with strong arms catches me. Or I can take the lead from Lady Godiva and ride naked down Adderley Street. Somewhere along the way I'm sure to find a chap who's kinky about cellulite and broken veins.'

'I agree with Griet,' said Nella. 'Good looks are still the easiest insurance policy against sleeping alone.'

'Easy?' asked Tienie, her eyebrows expressing pure indignation.

'Well, you're obviously not completely over the hill yet, Griet,' Nella consoled her. 'You seduced Adam, didn't you?'

'And if I remember correctly,' murmured Tienie into her beer, 'even Eve couldn't do that without the help of a snake.'

Giggling uncontrollably, Griet jumped up to let Petra in.

Petra wore a black and white outfit that sang 'New York, New York', gold earrings that seemed to hang down to her hips, and had her hair cut dead straight at her neck. She kissed her sisters European-style. She smelt of Marlboro and French perfume, thought Griet, still giggling as their cheeks touched.

'And how are you adapting?' asked Tienie. 'After a few days back in the Third World?'

'It's like riding a bike,' said Petra. 'Once you've lived here, you don't fall off.'

Griet escaped to the kitchen to laugh some more in front of the fridge.

The five journeyed on together, back to the castle from which the blowing stepmother had been driven. There they heard the king was offering half his fortune to anyone who could beat him in a race, and the fleet-footed brother immediately offered to compete against him.

The brother ran so much faster than the king that he was able to stop halfway for a snooze. Resting his head on a tree-stump, he fell fast asleep and the king overtook him. When the king was no more than a few paces from the winning post, the sharp-eyed sister saw where her brother was sleeping. She took up a gun and shot the tree-stump out from under his head. The brother woke in a fright and managed to beat the king to the finishing post in the nick of time.

The king was highly incensed at having to hand over half his fortune – and to the brother of a woman he'd driven from his castle. Just wait, he decided. I'll teach this wretched gang a lesson. He laid on a feast for them in a room with a steel floor and walls. When they sat down at table, he locked the iron door and ordered the cook to make a fire under the floor so that the whole room would get red hot.

'And what kind fairy should I thank for this invitation?' asked Marko in the kitchen door, grimacing as the incense hit him. 'You've lived like a hermit for months. I was beginning to suspect that you were growing cannabis, forging money or running an escort agency.'

'Sorry to disappoint you.' Griet passed him a beer from the fridge. 'The place depresses me so much I haven't wanted to expose anyone else to it.'

'What made you change your mind?'

'Father Time.' Griet smiled and gave him a bag of Niknaks to take to the living room. 'If you're patient, you can even get used to hell. But I must say I've been feeling much better since the day before yesterday when I signed for my own flat – like a prisoner who knows her sentence is almost over.'

'So, it's actually a farewell party?' asked Nella when Griet and Marko joined them again.

'Farewell to the flat and farewell to the year,' Griet nodded, sitting down on the floor beside Tienie. 'Both equally depressing.'

She'd decided yesterday to invite them for a sundowner. They'd all already made other plans for the rest of the evening. Like most people do on New Year's Eve, she thought self-pityingly. The past seven years she and her husband had always spent New Year's Eve with friends. This year her friends had obviously all forgotten her existence.

In no time at all, the five round the table grew so warm that one of them got up to open the door. Then they realized that the door was locked and the room was getting hotter and hotter. 'The king won't get rid of us this easily,' cried the clown, straightening her hat on her head. Immediately the temperature dropped so low that the drinks froze in their glasses.

When the king unlocked the door a few hours later to find the five still full of life, he was thunderstruck. The fire still blazed under the floor, but the room was ice cold. Right, decided the king, if I can't kill them, I must get them out of my kingdom some other way. Look, he said, instead of half my fortune, I'll give you my greatest treasure. The fast brother, he said, could marry his only daughter within a fortnight, and as a dowry they'd get as many treasures as one of the five could carry.

The blowing stepmother agreed immediately and summoned all the seamstresses in the kingdom. They had fourteen days to make the biggest sack in the world, she told them. When the wedding day dawned, the strong sister took the sack and went off to the king's treasure vaults where she gathered all the king's treasures. When all the vaults were empty, the sack wasn't even half full, and, laughing, she threw it over her shoulder and waved to the king as she left. 'Your daughter can decide for herself who she wants to marry,' the brother then told the king. 'But meanwhile she can come along with us and see the world.'

She'd almost wept with gratitude when Adam had phoned yesterday from his parents' place to say he'd be back tonight. And then she'd popped in on Gwen and landed an invitation for New Year's Eve.

'I should have invited you ages ago.' Gwen was clearly embarrassed. 'But I was sure you'd have something else on the go.'

It all went to show, thought Griet, and asked if she could bring Adam along.

'Of course. I'm dying to meet him.'

'I'm dying to meet him,' Petra told Marko.

'I don't know what you all expect of the poor chap,' snapped Griet. 'We're like chalk and cheese.'

'Opposites attract,' said Nella.

'Tell that to my husband.'

'Your ex-husband,' Tienie corrected her.

'He's not my ex-husband yet.'

'But you may as well start practising saying it,' suggested the always practical Petra.

'Anyway, you're the only one who wants to talk about your ex-husband,' said Nella. 'We're more interested in your new lover.'

'I don't think he's ever read a book in his life,' Griet said carefully.

'Don't you think that's part of your problem?' asked Nella. 'Do you really think a man has to read books to be a good lover?'

'Give Griet a break,' said Marko through a mouthful of Niknaks. 'She's always had a thing about intellectuals.'

'The gods punish people by making their wishes come true,' murmured Tienie.

Griet took a quick swig of wine and got up to go to the balcony.

'Look who's talking!' laughed Marko. 'You're just as big a snob about university degrees, Tienie.'

'No, now you're being unfair.'

'You're just as bad as each other, you and Griet, and all your intellectual friends. You use words you'd never hear in normal people's conversations. "Sycophant" and "pertinent" and "categorical".'

'And "deconstruct",' Griet chipped in from the balcony.

'Et tu, Brute?'

'It's true, Tienie,' said Griet with a shrug. 'I get just as irritated –'

'You hide behind words,' Marko interrupted her. 'Nothing that's happening in this country really affects you. You philosophize about it.'

'What's up with you?' asked Nella. 'Why are you so bloody-minded?'

'Is the army after you again?' asked Petra.

'Not to mention you two.' Marko was standing in the middle of the living-room floor like a boxer in a ring. 'Nella dresses up like a clown while everything's burning around her. And Petra simply retreated when things got too hot, hopping on the first plane to New York. There are lots of ways of hiding.'

His sisters stared after him as he walked out. Even Tienie was at a loss for words.

'Behind clothes, behind money, behind your husband's career . . .'

'Behind a camera?' asked Griet when he came to lean on the balcony railing beside her.

'Sure. I protect myself from the reality of a township. I take pictures of it. But you don't even know what reality is, Griet. You sit at a PC and write fairy tales.'

Griet looked past her brother's distressed eyes to the mountain that seemed much closer than usual this evening.

'Just you wait,' she said, holding out a hand to stop the mountain from climbing over the railings. 'One day I'm still going to write a story about reality.'

'And it'll probably also sound like a fairy tale,' said her brother.

As the five fellow travellers left his kingdom with all his treasure, the king flew into a terrible rage. He called up all the soldiers in the realm and commanded them to set off in pursuit and recover his fortune (and his only daughter). But the sister with the sight saw the soldiers from far off and warned the others.

No, no, no, thought the stepmother. This is no good. And she drew a deep breath and blew away the whole company of soldiers – horses and weapons and all. They landed in a great heap under the castle walls. When the king saw this, he realized that the five had something against which he was powerless, and he left them alone from that day on.

The five divided the treasure between them, giving the king's daughter a share as well. And each one made his or her own way in the world. The king's daughter decided not to be married to anyone. She went to live with the strong sister in the city of gold. Where they are most likely still living happily today.

18

Fee, Fie, Fo, Fum, I Smell the Blood of
a Human Child

TEARING HER hair out, was Griet's
first thought as she woke with Adam's hands in her hair.
In one of the books she'd borrowed from the library last
week, she'd read that one of the most pervasive beliefs
about witches was that their power lay in their hair. She
had no difficulty in believing that. She'd grown up with
the story of Samson.

She wished she could wake up every morning like this,
with Adam snuggled against her back, his hands in her
hair, his breath on her neck. *Le gros bon ange*, it was called
in the language of enchantment of the West Indies – the
soul that was revealed in the breath. The great good angel.

'I'm going to miss you,' she murmured without opening
her eyes.

She could feel his penis grow until he began to thrust
blindly between her legs, a seeking snout against her groin.
A lemming headed for oblivion, she thought, and felt him
hesitate for a moment on the edge of the precipice. Then
he crashed down into her. Her body was a pit, a deep dark
hole that men fell into, where children died, from whence
no one could ever be rescued. No, a cup, she thought, full,
fuller, fullest.

My cup runneth over.

That must be how the first woman felt. Eve, after she'd

brought shame, sex and sin into the world. Or the mythical Pandora who was destined to bring a box full of evil to humanity. Because Prometheus had stolen fire from the gods. Adam, Adam, Adam who could light the fire of the gods between a woman's legs.

'*Depilation of the witch frequently preceded torture. Once shorn of her bodily hair, it was thought that even the most obdurate of witches would make the confession required of her.*' No wonder, thought Griet when she opened her eyes and caught sight of the stubble sprouting in her armpit.

'Good morning, South Africa,' said Adam, kissing her shoulder.

'This can't be South Africa.' Griet smiled drowsily. 'It feels too good.'

He rolled her over so she was lying on her stomach. Their lower bodies stuck together with semen, he raised himself on his elbows to control his pelvis better. He glowed hotly inside her. The rubbing set her alight all over again. His lower body the bellows, the fire a blaze that even her blood couldn't quench. Adam, Adam, Adam, she crackled.

'Adam!' she shrieked.

His arms faltered, Samson's pillars, and the temple collapsed on to her back.

'You didn't use a condom,' she gasped when she could find breath to do so.

'You can't fall pregnant in the middle of your period.'

'That isn't what I worry about these days, my darling Adam,' she sighed, closing her eyes again. She didn't want to ruin the moment by mentioning the unmentionable. Who knew how many honey jars this golden organ had been thrust into?

'What does he do?' was Petra's first question.

That was the difference between her sisters, Griet realized. Nella asked what he looked like, Petra what he did and Tienie: How do you feel about him? Tienie and her therapist.

'I suspect he's a gigolo,' she said, just to get a reaction from Petra.

'Can you afford a gigolo?' was Petra's immediate response, more concerned about her sister's finances than her morals or her health.

'He looks like a gigolo,' she told Nella.

'Great! Then he'll know what to do in bed.'

'I don't know,' she told Tienie and her therapist. 'I'm trying to think less and do more.'

My sister wants to know what you do, Adam.

Tell her I'm searching for myself.

She'll want to know if you have a sponsor for your search. She'll offer to create an advertising campaign for you.

Tell her my hands are capable of anything.

As though I didn't know that, my darling Adam.

'He works in a restaurant sometimes,' she said finally so that Petra's great good angel could get some rest.

'Did it rain or was I dreaming?'

'It rained all night.' He rolled off her and folded his arms complacently behind his head. 'If you turn that delicious body of yours over, you'll see something that'll give you a big thrill.'

'You're impossible!'

'Oh come on, I don't mean me. Open your eyes and look outside.'

She turned on her side, still drowsy, and gasped for breath when she saw the rainbow framed by the window.

It seemed to have been painted on to the glass, an arch of enamelled colours, crystal clear. She raised herself on an elbow and stared at it.

'Does that mean we can't go to the mountain?' asked Adam, sounding genuinely disappointed.

'We could hike up – but that isn't what you had in mind, is it?'

Last night, in a moment of weakness under his supple

body, she'd confessed to the crazy fantasy of sex in a cable car. It had fired him up so much that he'd immediately invited her to give it a whirl with him on his last day in Cape Town. She knew it was useless arguing.

'It's just a fantasy, Adam.' She fell back on her pillow, her head in the hollow of his arm, her eyes on the rainbow. 'It shouldn't come true.'

'Hey, why not?'

'My sister Tienie says the gods punish us by making our wishes come true.'

'There's a difference between a wish and a fantasy. It's like, you know, wishes are impossible. I wish I was you, I wish I was a movie star, that sort of crap. But fantasy can come true. Fantasy should come true! It's like, something you can do, something you want to do, but don't have the guts for. It's like fucking a complete stranger in a train going through a tunnel! The stuff movies are made of!'

He put a hand under her chin, turned her face away from the window, forcing her to meet his eyes. His hand was bloodstained, she noticed. She didn't know whether she wanted to laugh or to cry.

'You should act out your fantasies,' he told her seriously.

'Do you?'

Silly question, she realized immediately. She could only hope it began to rain again.

'I'll tell you what: we'll go up at dusk. We'll watch the sunset, then come down again after dark. We'll probably be the only passengers. Maybe it'll be your lucky day!'

'Adam!'

'Go on, be a devil.'

With an angel in a cable car.

'Swing from a chandelier!'

That's probably how it would feel to have sex in a cable car.

'The only thing to fear is fear itself!'

Grandma Lina's granddaughter. She shut her mouth firmly before she could say another word. She rubbed her face against the wiry hair under his arm and his sweat was salty on her tongue. It looked as though the lower part of his body had been wounded. The man who feared nothing, she thought, not even a woman's blood.

Adam was one of those rare males who genuinely didn't give a damn if his body, or the sheets, or even his mouth, was soiled with menstrual blood. Oh, they all said they didn't mind, but see how they rushed off to the nearest washbasin the minute the orgasm had subsided. The proof of the pudding is in the eating.

If men menstruated, Gloria Steinem had dreamt, it would have been something to boast about. If horses could grow wings, Griet dreamt, a cow could jump over the moon. The mind of modern man was in revolt against his ancestors, but his soul was still in bondage.

Contact with menstrual blood was regarded as mortally dangerous in many primitive cultures. As a precaution, women were segregated, sometimes even locked up. According to Leviticus, it wasn't only the menstruating woman who was infected but also anything she sat or lay on for the next seven days. And anyone who touched her bed or anything she sat or lay on. And anyone who kept company with her and anything such a person sat or lay on . . .

'*In many places menstruating women have been prevented from touching the earth with their feet in case they should pollute the ground.*' Question: How does a woman get about if she may not touch the ground? Answer: She climbs on to a broom and starts to fly.

She waits until after dark and then she flies up through her chimney to the highest branches of a tree. Or she changes into a ball of fire, or into a nightbird, and she flies to a mysterious wood where she and her sisters turn their backs to one another and dance in the moonlight.

'Let's see what happens,' she said at last to Adam. 'Let's see what the weather does.'

'While the weather looks like this, we may as well just stay in bed.'

'Wonderful idea,' she answered with alacrity. 'I've got a lot of sleep to catch up on.'

'Hey, not a chance! It's your last day with me – do you think you're going to sleep?'

'The spirit is willing, darling Adam, but the flesh is weak.'

'So why don't you tell me a story?'

Was she imagining it or had the rainbow begun to fade?

If a witch was really stubborn, she read in her library book, if even a shaved body didn't persuade her to play ball, she was kept awake.

'*An iron bridle was bound across her face with four prongs thrust into her mouth. The "bridle" was fastened behind to the wall by a chain in such a manner that the victim was unable to lie down. In this position she was kept sometimes for several days – while men were constantly by to keep her awake.*'

'Once upon a time, long ago, there were three gods who sat on three thrones above the rainbow. The Mighty, the As Mighty and the Third Person . . .'

'I knew you wouldn't be able to resist the temptation!' Adam crowed, running his hand covered with dried blood through her hair.

At least it was less sexist than the Father, the Son and the Holy Ghost, she thought when Jans had told her the story of the Scandinavian gods.

Or the Father, the Son and the Holy Ancestors' Ghosts, as a *sangoma* had recently insisted on *Good Morning, South Africa*. God conveyed his wishes to Christ, explained the witch-doctor with three fingers in the air, who conveyed it to the *amadlozi* – the spirits of the forefathers – who in their turn passed it on to the *sangomas* and other mortals. No wonder the messages that eventually reached her on earth were so confusing, thought Griet. Brziffgtprkss.

'At last I know why I write fairy tales about my grand-parents,' she'd told her therapist that very morning. 'The *sangoma* reckons you can't ignore the spirits of your forefathers. They can drive you mad. They can even kill you.'

'Do you believe that?' Rhonda had asked very carefully.

'What's the alternative? Two men and a bird?'

As usual, Rhonda's face was a blank page upon which Griet could scrawl all her emotions in invisible ink.

'That's what Robertson Davies called the Trinity,' she added apologetically. 'Rhonda, if I knew what I believed, I wouldn't sit and torture myself here week after week.'

'One day the Third Person decided to go and see how the mortals dwelt on earth. Leaving her throne unattended, she made the long journey in the company of her sister, the Rain . . .'

She believed in the power of imagination, Griet decided, rather than the impotence of reality.

She believed in the possibility of love rather than the certainty of death.

She believed in stories . . . but was that enough?

Dizzy Tales

'An African witch can be young, because her evil powers and activities
have nothing to do with her age or
appearance. In fact, there is not much
she can do about her inherent wicked-
ness, though if she is lucky her supernatural powers will be quiescent, and
she will be able to live a normal life as
a member of her community.'

Encyclopaedia of Magic and Superstition

19

The Cook Who Wanted to Learn
How to Live

'*I USED THE* oven.' Pleased with herself, Griet leant back in the sucking chair. She wouldn't be swallowed, she knew now; she wouldn't disappear that easily from the face of the earth. Too bad if she had to peer out over her kneecaps at her therapist. 'To cook food.'

Rhonda nodded encouragingly.

'I made a farewell dinner for Adam. I was quite nervous because he's much more at home in the kitchen than I am. But I have this lasagne recipe that no one can mess up, not even me.'

Thank heaven for the Italians. Thank heaven for Italian fantasy and imagination, for Fellini and Bertolucci and Calvino and Moravia. Thank heaven for a country where the government changes every year, where a pope sets himself up as a king and a porn star is elected to parliament.

'Did you always have so little confidence as a cook, Griet?'

'No, I actually enjoyed it, long ago. Before the kitchen became a battlefield. With George every meal ended in an argument.'

By this time Adam was sleeping in the clouds somewhere over Africa. Like the angel she'd taken him to be that first night. Long ago mortals had to wait patiently for death before they could glimpse the glory of heaven. These days they hopped into the belly of an aircraft and had a preview, a heavenly sight-seeing tour, while girls with wings offered them drinks.

'I thought it only happened in cartoons – the volte-face of the married man – the thoughtful, obliging lover who is transformed into a seriously retarded baby. George brought me coffee in bed before we were married. It's no hassle, he said, he woke up earlier than I did anyway. In my whole married life, I never once got a cup of coffee in bed, not even when I was pregnant and felt like throwing up every time I tried to raise my head from the pillow. And I was pregnant the whole time, as you know.'

She lit a cigarette. To hell with discipline. The blue pools of Rhonda's eyes were as inscrutable as ever.

'When did you last see him?'

'Three days ago. Completely unexpectedly. If I think of how many times I've driven past his house in these last months! Or looked for excuses to pop in on someone who might have seen him. And when I finally stop wondering where he is and what he's up to, I bump into him in the last place I'd have expected. On the beach!'

Rhonda crossed her legs at the knee, something she very seldom did. Griet realized that she knew her therapist's body language as well as a close friend's. She knew every gesture and every expression on her face. Admittedly, it wasn't exactly an Italianate variety. And naturally she knew nothing of what was going on in her therapist's heart.

'George never went to the beach. He grew up in the Orange Free State – he's more frightened of the sea than my Grandma Lina was – and he always thought it was ridiculous to take your clothes off and sunbathe. Where he comes from, you'd probably be roasted to death if you did that. And there he was lying on Clifton beach like a rock-rabbit in the sun!'

'Well, he changed after you married, didn't he? He'll probably change again now that you're getting divorced. Haven't you changed too, Griet?'

'Not from Dr Jekyll into Mr Hyde! I don't know, I suppose I have. I'm more cynical than I was.'

'A healthy streak of cynicism can be a good thing.'

'But an overdose can kill you. Or at least kill all your emotions. In the end you can't love anyone any more.'

'And you think that's what happened to George?'

'God only knows what happened to George,' sighed Griet with her eyes on Mickey Mouse's crippled arms. 'I think he sold his soul to the devil.'

Rhonda wrote something in the file on her lap. She was wearing a pale blue silk shirt, the same colour as her eyes, and shoes that could only be Italian. The caramel-coloured leather looked like creased satin. The sort of shoes a modern Cinderella would wear. You couldn't walk down a modern pavement in glass slippers. Thank heaven for the Italians.

'Did you speak to each other?'

'On the beach? We said hello. He was with some other people and I was with Adam.'

It was more embarrassing than she'd admit. She had to pluck up all her courage to be seen at Clifton beside Adam's heavenly body. She couldn't bear to think what she looked like beside him with her winter-white skin and her voluptuous hips. What if someone thought she was his mother? she thought in a panic. If all else failed, she comforted herself, she could always expose her breasts to distract attention from her thighs.

Her breasts had always been her strong point. Not as strong as her brain, obviously. Though lately she'd developed a horrible suspicion her breasts had begun to droop, and she had her doubts about her brain as well. Unavoidable, certainly, after a succession of pregnancies and seven years with a clever man.

And then she'd bumped into George on the beach. If she'd come upon him in heaven, it would have surprised her less. She had just spread her towel out on the sand and undone the clasp on her top. She was luckily still lying on her stomach – compelled to modesty by the perfect teenage nipples on all sides – when she saw him sitting on a rock opposite. He must have noticed her, she thought, hot with embarrassment. He must have noticed Adam's hand on her bare back. One of the women in his group was a stranger to her. Irrationally she hoped that he'd slept with this woman recently. Anything to ease her own feeling of guilt.

But even stranger than this odd wish was the feeling of alienation. She still loved him, she realized, but it was the sort of love you store away somewhere in your heart for someone who is dead. She would always love the man he was long ago. The reddish body over there on the rock, laughing with a strange woman, was someone she didn't know.

'And what about Adam?'

'What about Adam?' Griet smiled idiotically. 'What do you want to know?'

'How do you feel about . . . what happened?'

What her therapist wanted to know was whether she'd slept with the man. She decided to be enigmatic – or as enigmatic as you could be with someone who knew your filthiest thoughts.

'I'm not sorry.'

It wasn't so easy to smile like the Mona Lisa with someone you'd used as your personal confessor for months. Naturally she still felt guilty, but she'd also learnt that guilt could be a more powerful aphrodisiac than seafood.

'Three months without a man', she had written yesterday in her Creative Arts Diary. And then she'd scratched the words out and written: 'Three months without my ex-husband.'

'What do you want to happen next, Griet?'

'With Adam?'

'With your life in general . . .'

What would she like to happen next, Griet wondered while she stared thoughtfully at her kneecaps, or at the floral dress that hung in folds over her kneecaps. She wanted a good fairy, or one of her grandfather's angels, or the Egyptian goddess Aridia, mother of witches, to make all her wishes come true. She wanted the world to believe in something again. She wanted to write fairy tales. But that wasn't what her shrink wanted to hear.

The ghastly country where our heroine lived, she was going to write tonight in her book with the beautiful pages, was a place where everything was forbidden. The king had forbidden the truth, and the pages of many newspapers had bare patches, bare as the king's head, and white as the queen's thighs. (Which no one but the king had ever seen, of course.) When the truth had first been forbidden, the people clutched desperately at fantasy and imagination, and so the bald king decided to forbid fantasy and imagination too. He shut down the libraries and the theatres and changed the art galleries into prisons.

Humour was all the people had left. They could laugh at the country they lived in, at the queen's white thighs and the bare newspapers and the art gallery prisons, and they could laugh at their powerlessness to do anything but laugh. Then the king decided to forbid humour, and he threw all the clowns into the art gallery prisons, and all the banana peels into the sea, and forbade the people to laugh at anything but his own feeble jokes about other countries.

'I want people to laugh at everything that's absurd,' Griet admitted to her kneecaps. 'From politics to the power of the penis.'

'And you yourself?' Rhonda wanted to know.

'I've been laughing at myself for months already.'

'No, what I mean is: What do you want for yourself, Griet?'

'You can't take yourself seriously any more once you have a failed suicide attempt behind you. I know now that I can survive everything, even the cockroaches in my friend's flat. Even the stupid armchairs in my shrink's consulting room.'

Griet's head jerked up when a strange noise came from Rhonda's throat, like breaking glass. Her therapist had burst into tears! Rhonda's composed face suddenly looked sloppy, crumpled, her mouth gaping and her head thrown back. No, she realized, her therapist was laughing.

This is what Rhonda must look like when she was having an orgasm, Griet realized.

It was over in a minute, as suddenly as it had begun. Rhonda rubbed her eyes, gasped for breath, and rearranged her features neatly.

'You can't always laugh,' said Rhonda as calmly as ever. 'You have to be able to cry too.'

Griet stared at her therapist. Rhonda's legs were crossed at the ankle as usual, her back straight on the red sofa, her hands folded on the file on her lap. Griet thought of her grandmother. After she'd caught her up a tree, she'd seen her through new eyes. But Grandma Lina had looked exactly as before, with her down-at-heel shoes and her plaited bun. Or was it all just a figment of Griet's imagination?

'I cried non-stop day and night for three months!' she exclaimed. 'And then I stuck my head in an oven. And when I couldn't even make a success of that, I began to laugh. Kundera says the devil laughs about the senseless-ness of everything and the angels laugh about how wonder-ful it all is. I laugh with the devil — and to hell with the rest!'

'Can't you laugh with the devil *and* the angels?'

'Running with the hare and hunting with the hounds?'

Rhonda shook her head. A hint of a laugh-line still lingered at the corner of her mouth.

'My grandmother was afraid of everything,' said Griet, and her eyes began to sting. 'But she could climb trees. I can laugh.'

20

Clever Gretchen Greets the Golden Goose

YOU COULD see from Jans's house that its master had given his heart to Africa. Framed black-and-white photographs of township children toyi-toying, funeral crowds with clenched fists and policemen throwing tear-gas decorated the bathroom walls. Striped mats made in the Transkei were scattered on the stripped wooden floors and the second-hand sofa was covered with cushions embroidered with lizards. Carved walking sticks from Malawi waited in a drum near the front door for anyone who fancied a walk.

'Food's nearly done,' said Jans at the stove, taking a swig from the wine bottle which he kept close at hand in the interests of the culinary art.

'You've been saying that for hours,' complained Gwen with her elbows on the dining-room table. 'We'll be so tiddly by the time we get to eat we won't be able to taste anything.'

Jans was roasting a leg of mutton that Gwen had brought from her parents' farm. As the walls between the kitchen, dining room and living room had been removed, he could talk to his guests while fulfilling his duties as chef. He lifted the lid of a casserole and the aroma drifted to the dining room on the stirring notes of Janacek's 'Taras Bulba'. Jans closed his eyes and sniffed ecstatically.

'Mint and orange,' he sighed.

Griet met Gwen's eyes and shook her head. 'I've never seen anyone have such a jol in the kitchen.'

'May one ask where Klaus is tonight?' asked Jans, opening the oven door to take the roast out.

The aroma overwhelmed his two guests. They sat at a rough old yellowwood table that had been used for years in his grandmother's farm kitchen. A toy wire-and-tin windmill stood in the middle of the table in place of the conventional vase of flowers.

'One may,' Gwen told him, 'but one won't get an answer from me.'

Jans carved the meat, arranging the pink slices on a large platter. He brought it to the table like a father carrying a child to the font at a christening.

'I'm going to move out,' said Gwen once they'd raved sufficiently over Jans's prowess as a cook. 'I can't stay with Klaus any longer.'

Griet and Jans exchanged a quick glance, but Gwen avoided meeting their eyes. None of them knew what to say next. They listened to 'Taras Bulba' in silence.

It wouldn't be the first time that Gwen and Klaus had broken up.

'Well . . .' said Jans when the silence started getting uncomfortable.

'Are you certain?' asked Griet carefully. 'The other times . . .'

'Of course I'm not certain,' Gwen told them through a mouthful of meat. 'I've been saying it for a year, every time I have too much to drink. And next day I stay put because I'm afraid of being alone.'

'The old Goths believed that all important matters must be discussed twice, Gwen,' Jans told her. 'Once while you're drunk to ensure passion and once when you're sober to ensure discretion.'

'My passion says to me: Get the hell out of it; my discretion says: Wait, maybe there's still hope. Everyone says you know when a relationship is over. *How* do you know? That's what I ask myself. Is it like a bolt of lightning that strikes you, scales falling from your eyes, waking up one day and knowing? How did *you* know, Griet?'

'I woke up one day with my head in the oven. Then I knew.'

'Maybe one should stay drunk,' laughed Gwen. 'Who wants to be discreet? Can I have some more wine, please?'

Had she become such a clown, wondered Griet, that no one believed her when she was serious any more? She looked at the flower-patterned porcelain plate before her, something else Jans's grandmother had left to him. All she'd inherited from her grandparents, she thought rebelliously, were personality defects.

Perhaps she shouldn't laugh so much, as her analyst had suggested. That way her family and friends might realize she wasn't waving to them, she was waving her arms to chase the wolf away. Or was the wolf also only a figment of her imagination?

'Do you know there's a bird called a *swartstertgriet*?' asked Jans out of the blue.

Griet and Gwen looked at each other and burst out laughing.

'No, I didn't know, Jans, but thank heavens I won't go to my grave without that bit of information.'

'*Limosa limosa*: rare migrant, fond of water. Black-tailed godwit.'

'*Godwit*?' Griet shook her head incredulously. 'Is that what they call a Griet in English?'

'The only *swartstertgriet* that I've ever heard of,' said Gwen, topping up all three glasses, 'is the one you drink out of.'

'No, Gwen, that's *swartgriet*! As in kissing *swartgriet*. That's the expression for drinking too much, isn't it?'

'Oh. Well, seeing we're talking about birds, have you heard from the golden goose?'

'OK, make a joke of it. He was good for me.'

'Adam?' asked Jans, helping himself to a second serving as large as the first.

'Did you know that the original story of Hansel and Gretel ended with the children climbing on to the back of a goose?'

'What are you trying to say, Gretel?' Jans looked at her over the top of his spectacles, his eyes more serious than usual.

'If you can't get a horse to be your Pegasus, maybe you could use a goose?'

'A goose might be more suitable,' said Jans, 'in your case.'

'Why?' she asked suspiciously.

'A horse symbolizes war, and I gather you're tired of making war?'

'And what would a goose symbolize?' Griet smiled at Jans. 'Nursery rhymes?'

'There are lots of ways of flying,' said Jans. 'Isn't that what you're trying to say?'

'Well, have you heard from him again?' Gwen still wanted to know.

'No, and I don't expect ever to do so.' She took a generous swig of wine. 'What could he say to me? Hey, man, I love you, baby?'

Gwen looked down at her plate, rubbing a hand over her cropped hair.

'More meat for anyone?' asked Jans, making for the kitchen.

'I wonder if I'll ever sleep with a man,' said Griet, with her eyes still on the table in front of her, 'without falling in love just a tiny bit. I know I'm not supposed to admit it. I'm a liberated woman, aren't I?'

Gwen clicked her tongue and refilled Griet's glass.

'I know it's ridiculous. Adam talks like a surfer and thinks like a teenager. But his body . . .'

Griet twirled a strand of hair round her finger. Adam's body was fluent in the seven languages of heaven. And her body wanted to answer him in all seven. '*Women who scream and shout,*' she'd read in the paper, '*are likely to live longer, healthier lives.*' Thank you, Adam, she thought. '*According to researchers from the University of Michigan, "polite" women who swallow their anger are three times more likely to die young than their more extrovert sisters.'* If she could just escape Aids and cancer and the oven, she could probably still live a long and healthy life.

'He made me feel safe. God, do you know how good it feels to lie beside a man who's afraid of nothing?' She rubbed her eyes. 'I'm starting to get maudlin. I miss him at night, I want to close my eyes and snuggle in under his arm. I'm tired of lying alone and afraid in my bed.'

Jans brought the platter back to the table with a fresh load of meat.

'Eat, Griet. It'll make you feel better.'

He smoothed her hair; a clumsy gesture that brought tears to her eyes.

'Sorry.' She linked her hands in front of her forehead, elbows on the table, so they wouldn't see her eyes. 'Since my shrink told me yesterday that I shouldn't laugh so much, I just want to cry the whole time.'

'Drink,' said Gwen, raising her glass to Griet. 'I feel as though I want to have a good cry myself. Klaus hates it. It makes him feel helpless. He hates feeling helpless.'

'I can't cry in front of other people.' Griet swallowed the lump in her throat. 'It's false pride, I know. I inherited my grandfather's false pride and my grand-mother's fears. And a good dose of Calvinism to fuck me up thoroughly. But in private I cry like an actress in a Greek tragedy.'

'Don't we all?' asked Gwen.

But there was something in her, Griet knew in her heart, that remained aloof even when she wept, even when she was alone, perhaps especially when she was alone. When her face crumpled and her cheeks were stained with tears, the storyteller in her watched, fascinated by the sobbing Griet Swart.

That was the worst thing about being a storyteller. She became an observer of her own life.

'I think you all try too hard to be tough.' A sudden

silence fell and Jans jumped up to change the record. 'You make us poor males feel quite inadequate.'

Griet closed her eyes and relaxed back in her chair to listen to Mozart.

'Who do you mean by "you"?' demanded Gwen, gesticulating so vehemently that her wine slopped on to the table. 'What the hell do *you* want? Every time I open my heart to a man, the door is slammed in my face!'

Jans looked flustered.

'It's as though you're encouraging us to be dishonest. As though you're so used to being manipulated that you run away if a woman tells you frankly what she wants.'

Griet went through to the living room and picked up the record cover. Symphony No. 41 in C Major. 'Jupiter'.

'Do you really want us to play games for the rest of our lives?' Gwen asked in a voice that suddenly sounded weary. She leant back in her chair, exhausted by her own anger. 'Don't show that you're crazy about him, it'll scare him off. Don't say you want children, it'll make him impotent.'

Griet's eyes started to sting again. She was tired of cynicism and just as tired of idealism. She was tired of irony and absurdity and humour, tired of laughing when she really felt like crying. Tired of living when she really wanted to be dead.

'If you don't act tough, Jans,' said Gwen quietly, 'you land on your arse.'

They listened to the music in silence until Jans asked at last, 'Well, what *do* you want?'

'Just listen to this.' Griet brought the record cover back to the table. '"*All four movements are based on the principle of a dualistic union between masculine strength and feminine tenderness — expressed as a dialogue between wind and string instruments in perfect harmony.*"'

'Ha, ha, ha,' said Gwen without a smile.

'What do you want, Griet?' asked Jans, leaning towards her.

He looked as though he'd wiped his mouth with newspaper; as though he hadn't seen a razor for ages.

Did he really want to know what she wanted?

'I'd like to say to Adam: Hey, come on, live with me and be my love. I know it wouldn't work, but it's a great fantasy. If I could transplant someone else's head on to his body, I'd be the happiest woman on earth.'

'For a few weeks,' smiled Gwen.

'Is that too much to ask?'

Jans shook his head as though he couldn't believe his ears. Griet looked at the framed poster above the dining-room table. *Mayibuye iAfrika*. Where would her help come from, she wondered. Wishes didn't come true any more and fantasy was a horse of a different colour, not one she could fly away on. She sighed heavily as the third move-ment of Mozart's symphony began.

'But you can't really take a guy in a pair of Union Jack underpants too seriously,' said Griet.

'*What?*' asked Gwen.

'He's got this thing about funny underpants.' She shrugged. 'He's got a pair with Uncle Sam pointing his finger and saying: "I want YOU".'

Gwen bit her lip to stop herself from laughing. Jans dropped his head into his hands and studied the empty plate in front of him with apparent interest.

'And you, Jans?' She smiled at him when he dared to look up again. 'What do you want? And I'm not talking about politics.'

'Do I ever talk about politics to you?' He sounded peeved. 'Unless you ask me?'

'No, dear Jans, and you never laugh at my stupid questions. You're the nicest man I know.'

'Uncle Sam!' Gwen was shaking with laughter. 'I can't imagine Klaus in a pair of Uncle Sam underpants.'

'Nobody's perfect,' said Griet, relaxing back in her chair and allowing 'Jupiter' to wash over her.

21

Cat and Mouse Keep House

'IT'S A GOOD thing I arrived in time to help you with your Great Trek,' said Griet's sister Petra, wrapping a pile of plates in newspaper.

Griet looked up bemusedly from the saucepans ranged on the kitchen floor. Petra sat cross-legged amid a mountain of boxes, in her oldest designer T-shirt and faded Levi's, her beautifully manicured nails varnished rose pink. She looked like a princess playing housey-housey.

'I don't know if you're going to be able to believe this, Petra, but somehow I coped without you for a whole year.'

Petra raised her eyebrows. Griet could read her mind: in the last few years, her scatterbrained older sister had not only made a botch-up of three pregnancies, but she'd also lost a very presentable husband and a house designed by a yuppie architect. Not exactly a success story.

Griet got up and shoved the saucepans into a box. Now all she had to do was pick her cutlery from the jumble in the drawer, and then she'd be finished with this kitchen. For ever, she realized, and relief changed to despair.

What had happened to her glasses? Had George got so drunk every night that the glass fell out of his hand? Or had he smashed all the glasses in a single fit of rage?

No, thought Griet, George didn't have a sufficiently Greek temperament for that. She was the glass-smasher in their house. She was the one who lost control of her emotions, throwing things and slamming doors. Finally even hitting her husband.

She'd slapped his face one night, blind, deaf and dumb with rage, and then pounded him with her fists. It was definitely a low point in her life – nearly as low as the oven episode. If she were to compare low points.

And George had just stood there as though he were carved from stone, his face expressionless, no shock or disappointment or even satisfaction at her pathetic outburst. If only he'd wanted to hit her back! But George would never let himself go like that. George would never hit anyone, she realized that night with devastating certainty. The only emotion he had displayed during their seven years together was sometimes to groan slightly more loudly during an orgasm. And that time he smashed the car window. And that one time, long ago, when he'd wept.

It was when Griet had decided enough was enough and moved in with one of her girl friends. She'd scarcely had time to dry her eyes before she was involved with another man. It was nothing more than a crutch to lean on during those first unbearable months without George. But George reacted like a child who has discarded a toy and then desperately wants it back when he sees another child playing with it.

He rang her three times a day. He invited her to the most expensive restaurants in town. He even sent her flowers. As a last resort, he hammered on her friend's front door late one night.

'I love you, Griet,' he mumbled when she finally opened the door. He was flopped against the doorjamb and his breath smelt of whisky. 'I want to marry you. I want to have a child with you.'

She didn't know what to say. Her heart wanted him. Her body wanted him.

'Why do you have to drink yourself into a stupor before you can tell me this, George?'

'I love you.'

And then he wept. She opened the door wider and allowed him in. What woman could resist a weeping man?

That was how her unfortunate marriage began, with booze and tears, and that's how it dragged on. The wife had cried buckets in this house. The man had drunk buckets.

'Right.' Petra got up to rinse the newspaper ink from her hands. 'What next?'

If Petra's ambitious husband hadn't decided to study in New York, Griet would never have landed up in a depressing flat with a lethal gas oven and blocked drains. If Petra hadn't wanted to take a bite of the Big Apple, she would have arranged a proper place to stay for her sister long ago. Petra could lay on polar bears in the Sahara and camels in Antarctica. Just give her a telephone and a day or two.

Now she'd pitched up on holiday unexpectedly, just in time to organize her sister's emotional and physical move. *Deus ex machina*, thought Griet gratefully, if there ever was such a thing. She rang George's attorney – Griet simply hadn't been able to scrape together the courage to do it – and it had only taken her a couple of minutes to arrange that they should come and pack Griet's things today.

'But a day isn't long enough,' Griet had protested. 'We're talking about the possessions of seven years.'

'A day will be enough if I help you,' was Petra's determined answer. 'Come on, Griet, you aren't Elize Botha moving out of Tuynhuys.'

'It isn't as though I can walk in there and chew through the house like a caterpillar. I have to sort out my towels and leave his behind. We don't have His-and-Hers sets.'

'You can sort and I'll pack. And then we'll ask Marko and one of your strong men friends to come and help us load.'

'I don't have strong men friends,' Griet said despondently.

'I'm only talking about a couple of muscles, Griet,' Petra sighed. 'You must know someone with a couple of muscles?'

Tienie had muscles, thought Griet, but she was hibernating somewhere in a beach house with her new lover.

In the end she asked Jans. He had muscles and he was reliable.

'Now for the books,' said Griet, dragging her feet unwillingly to the living room.

'I'll just make sure all the boxes are securely fastened,' called the practical Petra.

Perhaps it was a good thing that she was granted a few minutes on her own in front of the wall-to-wall bookcase in her living room. This was the most difficult task of the day. A bookcase is the heart of a house, she'd always believed, whether it was a plank and brick affair in a student flat or an impressive wall unit in a designer residence. When you took the books away, the heart stopped beating.

'Come on, Griet, there's no time to stand and mope,' her sister said behind her.

Griet took a couple of paperbacks off the lowest shelf. Shakespeare's sonnets and a handful of her best-loved Frenchwomen: Colette and Simone de Beauvoir and Anaïs Nin. The diaries of Virginia Woolf, the poems of Sylvia Plath. And it wasn't all coppice wood that she'd find on these shelves either. Everything she'd ever wanted to know about angels: *Paradise Lost, Revolt of the Angels, The Book of Laughter and Forgetting*. Each volume a voyage of discovery to her own heart.

'Did this place ever make you really happy?' asked her sister, pulling a stout box closer.

'It isn't the house's fault that I wasn't happy.' She passed another handful of French books to Petra. Camus, she noticed. Naturally. 'I was crazy about this house, about the spiral staircase and the attic room and the squirrels in the garden. If George and I couldn't be happy together here, we couldn't be happy together anywhere.'

'But George has been threatening for years to sell the whole caboodle.'

'George will always put the blame for his own personality on to something else. It was always either the house or I that made him gloomy. The house was an easier scapegoat: it didn't answer back.'

Griet shook her head over four library books George's sons had taken out shortly before she left. Nearly half a year ago. Maybe she wasn't the most exemplary wife in the world, but she had at least seen to it that the children returned their library books on time.

'Do you think he'll sell it now?'

'I think he knows, in his heart of hearts, he'll be unhappy in any house.' Griet felt anxious all over again about the children's welfare when they spent weekends here. Their father hadn't taken them to the library for six months. How was she to know whether he gave them enough to eat? 'I think he feels less threatened now that I've gone.'

'Until the next woman moves in and makes everything unbearable again?'

'I don't know, I'm furious about being kicked out, but maybe I should be grateful that I'm the one who can escape all the unpleasant memories.'

Griet fetched a chair from the dining room so she could reach the books on the highest shelves. Every room in this house was a battlefield in an extended war, she realized. The long dining-room table was a trench in which they'd spent hours of silence, the double bed in the bedroom little better than a minefield. The kitchen was the scene of the fiercest assaults, where she'd bombarded him with screamed accusations and he'd tried to force her to surrender with annihilating arguments.

They were so obsessed that they didn't even spare the bathroom. Long ago they'd sometimes had sex behind a closed bathroom door, the shower taps open full to fool the children. In the last months they'd employed the same tactics to drown out the endless arguments. And in the end they hadn't hidden either the sex or the rows from the children.

Children are not as easily deceived as adults, Griet had learnt. They didn't have any problems believing in Santa Claus or talking animals, but they knew when you were trying to make out you were happily married.

'I don't believe it!' Petra picked up a tattered *War and Peace*, its cover repaired with tape. 'I thought this book was like *The Satanic Verses*. People like to keep it in the house to impress their friends, but just try to find someone who has read it from cover to cover. I swear this is the first time I can see anyone's read it.'

'I've also read *Don Quixote*,' said Griet. 'Do you think it's because I'm an oldest child?'

'It's probably got something to do with your horoscope.' Petra shook her head as she packed the book. 'Only someone who has struggled through *War and Peace* would endure seven years in a toxic relationship.'

'*What* kind of relationship?'

'Toxic,' said her sister, who believed in Linda Goodman's astrology and *Cosmopolitan*'s psychology. 'Couples who poison each other. Like Elizabeth Taylor and Richard Burton in *Who's Afraid of Virginia Woolf*.'

I am, thought Griet, I'm afraid. And not just of Virginia Woolf and her watery death. Can't a poisonous relationship also be a kind of suicide? *Look Back in Anger*?

'You get ordinary people,' she tried to explain, more to herself than to her sister, 'and you get obsessional people. Obsessional people smoke too much or drink too much or . . .'

'Get up in the middle of the night to scrub floors?'

Griet looked down at Petra, who resembled Grandma Lina more closely than any of the Swart sisters. Dark hair, dark eyes and olive skin. Not quite white, the family had whispered when she was young. Petra's reputation in the advertising industry was just as important to her as having the whitest washing in the street had been to Grandma Lina. But she hadn't inherited her grandmother's fears, thought Griet. Those had been destined for the oldest sister.

In the fairy tale about the twelve princesses who danced the shoes right off their feet every night, the youngest was the timid sister, the one who got premonitions and heard strange noises. The oldest sister had disappeared through the gap in the floor fearlessly, eager to go and dance underground.

But long ago she'd also been fearless, Griet remembered. Life had made her frightened.

'Do you think I take after Grandma Lina?'

'You live your obsessions out in another way, Griet.'

That was the difference between her and Adam, she realized. He lived out his fantasies and she lived out her obsessions. She got down from the chair with an armful of collections that she wanted to pack personally: *Die Volledige Sprokies van Grimm*, *The Complete Brothers Grimm Fairy Tales*, *Die Märchen der Brüder Grimm*, so she'd know where they were when she needed them. She looked up surprised when her sister took her arm.

'I wish we could have stopped you,' Petra said quietly. 'Before it was too late.'

'You couldn't have done anything.'

Even Louise couldn't stop her shutting her eyes tightly and leaping over the chasm.

'Face the facts, Griet. You've got one of those long relationships that's going nowhere,' Louise had warned her long ago, one of the few people who knew her well enough to be perfectly candid. 'Except perhaps backwards. I know what I'm talking about, Griet. I learnt my lesson with my own disastrous marriage.'

'You can't compare relationships,' said Griet stubbornly.

That was the last time Louise said anything critical about her friend's relationship.

> The most wonderful thing happened to me today [Louise wrote from London], and not a day too soon. I have been seriously considering poisoning my husband this last week. It's easy with the ghastly coffee we get here, he wouldn't even

taste the difference if I stirred arsenic into it. Otherwise I could shove him into the Thames. If he doesn't drown, a couple of mouthfuls of that filthy river water should be as good as poison.

I got a letter from Randy Rony. Remember that insatiable Israeli I had a fling with in Rome in my salad days? We met on the Spanish Steps and screwed just about everywhere except inside the Sistine Chapel. For years afterwards I wouldn't touch men who weren't circumcised. Well, he's based in Hong Kong now, and he's coming to London for some conference later this year. '*I'll never forget you,*' he writes, '*and the things you did to me! I'd love to see you again.*'

Griet and her husband even fought in the nursery. They'd even fought *over* the nursery. He'd suggested that she and the baby should sleep in the study on the top floor so that he wouldn't be disturbed at night. She'd told her friends as though it were a joke. She didn't realize he was serious.

When she was eight months pregnant, her gynaecologist assured her that nothing could go wrong now. She began to believe that, like most other women, she was capable of giving birth.

It was time to get the baby's room ready. She'd read somewhere that yellow walls can make a child happy. Silly, she thought, and went off to buy yellow paint. She was prepared to sell her soul to the devil for her child's happiness. Why not try yellow walls too? She put an overall over her enormous stomach and began painting one of the three bedrooms on the ground floor yellow.

George was sprawled on the sofa in front of the TV set. Maybe the programme was even worse than the usual fare; something must have disturbed him before he appeared behind her in the doorway.

'Since you insist on making life totally miserable for me,' he said in tortured tones, 'I'll sleep in the study on the top floor from now on.'

Don't allow yourself to get upset, she admonished herself as she painted on, it isn't good for an unborn baby.

'I don't expect you to get up if the baby cries at night,' she said with her back to him. 'But it would be nice if you were somewhere in the vicinity.'

'You know I battle with insomnia! It'll be unbearable for me to hear a child screaming.'

'All fathers think it's unbearable in the beginning.' The hand with the brush was suspended motionless in mid-air, but she managed to keep her voice calm. 'You'll get used to it.'

'I already have two children, Griet.'

She didn't trust her voice to say any more.

'You are the one who wanted this one,' he said and stalked off. 'It's your responsibility.'

The brush was hanging at her side and the yellow paint dripped on to her canvas shoes. She gazed at the half yellow wall before her wondering what to do. What does a woman do when her husband tells her that the baby who's to be born in a month's time is *her* responsibility?

She could bawl him out. She could run after him and pummel him with her fists. She could try to force him to take responsibility for something that happened to him, just for once in his life. But she had to stay calm for the sake of the unborn baby. She squatted down on her haunches and began to cry.

I've gone right overboard [wrote Louise]. I really want to pick up the fling where we left it ten years ago, but I'm simply not the nymph I was then. He'll die of shock if he sees me naked. I mean, we all have cellulite on our thighs, but I've got it on my ankles! I can't even remember whether I ever had a waist. And my stomach hangs in these loose folds; like floppy pancakes, just less appetizing.

And who knows what the hell has become of him? He's probably changed so much that I won't even recognize him. He's probably turned into a seedy businessman in a polyester suit. Bald, with a paunch. Not that I deserve anything else with my cellulite. On the one hand I almost hope he's become revolting, then I don't have to feel so bad about my own deterioration. But just picture it, Griet: me with my cellulite and my flabby stomach and he with his bald head and his paunch meeting in a hotel room to try and relive the passion of our youth!

A la recherche du temps perdu!

Thank heaven, thought Griet with a pile of children's books in her arms, she'd emptied out the nursery months ago. Returned the borrowed crib and pram, removed the framed pictures and the pinboard, packed the toys and most of the books into boxes. The baby clothes had been carefully folded in a suitcase. One of her sisters would need them one day, she consoled herself. All that remained of the nursery were the sunny yellow walls.

'*Dr Seuss's Sleepbook*!' Petra yelped. 'It was one of my favourites before I went to school!'

'If you ever have a baby one day, I'll give you all my children's books. I'll regard it as my duty. If it depended on you and François, the poor kid would only get the *Wall Street Journal* to read.'

'Come on, Griet, if it depended on you, the child would get more books than food!'

'Maybe not altogether a bad thing.'

Most of the books on the next shelf belonged to her husband. Politics and logic, she thought gloomily, that was all that was going to be left behind in this house. And unpleasant memories.

But just suppose he hasn't turned into a seedy businessman [Louise wrote yearningly]. What if he's just as attractive as ever? What if he's only become a little short-sighted (or even blind) so he'll find me attractive too? What if I leave my husband and he his wife (he must be married) and we go to Hong Kong together and live happily ever after?

Or at least until the colony reverts to China in a few years. There's no such thing as for ever and ever any more, is there?

22

How Many Princesses Can Dance on the Point of a Needle?

ONCE UPON a time there lived a shepherd's son who became famous far and wide because he had a good answer for any question he was asked. When a princess asked him how many drops of water there were in the sea, he answered, 'If the king stopped all the rivers so that not one more drop of river water flowed into the sea, I'd be able to tell you how many drops there are in the sea.'

George Moore grew up in the Orange Free State, the youngest of three sons of a woman who'd trained as a music teacher and a father who'd left school in Standard Six and gone to work on the farm. His mother was an angel, everyone said, but, like many angels, she didn't like people to touch her. Not even her own children. His father would have been happy to hug his sons, but fathers weren't supposed to touch their sons much. And his sons were scared of him because his breath stank of drink and the devil. George spent his life trying to balance on the fence between these two personalities. The chill of the soul and the fever of the body.

He was the apple of his mother's eye. He was cleverer than the others, better-looking, and he was the one she expected most of. She taught him to read before he turned four. He'd go far, she predicted, he just mustn't expect too much happiness. Happiness was reserved for sinners like his father.

He was a loner in the little school on the farm, too clever for the others in his class. After the first term, the teacher pushed him up to the next class. Then he was even more lonely because his classmates were all much older, than he was. After a year his mother decided to send him to a larger school far away from the farm. This meant that from a very early age he had to stay in a hostel.

He was a skinny child with hair that just wouldn't lie flat. He was only allowed home for two weekends each term. The first weekend at home he cried, but his mother looked so wounded that he never cried in front of her again, not even years later at her deathbed.

When the time came to go to high school, his mother sent him to one of the best boys' schools in the country. Each holiday he found less and less to say to his brothers, who'd all gone to school closer to home, and to his father who warmed himself up in the pub in town every evening because his own house had grown so chilly. His mother brought George coffee in the morning, and then sat on his bed and chatted about everything that had happened during the last term on the farm and in the district. And she always asked him what he was going to be one day.

She wanted him to become a powerful politician, rubbing shoulders with kings and presidents. Or a judge deciding about life and death. Or a brilliant surgeon performing operations that no one had even dreamt possible – like transplanting hearts or lungs.

His father wanted him to take over one of the family farms. Or go into business and make money.

At university, further from home than ever before, the world of the intellect really opened for George Moore for the first time. In the third week he travelled upwards and passed through the gates of a philosophical heaven. He never came back down to earth again. By the second year he'd read *The Fall* thirteen times and stopped believing in a god. If he'd believed in heroes, Camus would have been his hero.

Once he'd acquired a couple of degrees, he went to Europe to continue his studies and to think more freely. He said goodbye to his family on the farm as though he'd see them again within a year, but he didn't mean to come back. His mother read him like a book and she was the only one who suspected the truth. She wrote to him every week, about the weather and the neighbours and everything that had happened on the farm and in the district, but never asked when he'd be home.

When the princess asked the shepherd's clever son how many stars there were in heaven, he took a sheet of paper and a pen and made so many tiny dots on it that they swam before her eyes. Then he said, 'As many dots as there are on this sheet of paper, that's how many stars there are in heaven – you count them.'

George met his first wife in Europe, an English-speaking girl from his own country who'd been sent overseas by her prosperous parents to save her from marriage to a socially unacceptable man. And then she came back with a man who was even less acceptable: an Afrikaner.

His sojourn overseas was a sobering experience for George. He didn't have enough money; he often went to bed hungry; the cold winter weather got him down; the people's strange habits confused him. That was the beginning of the cynicism that lay heavier and heavier on his heart each year for the rest of his life.

After less than a year he was back in his own country, without completing his studies and with a pregnant English-speaking girl at his side. Her parents swallowed their colonial pride and organized a quick wedding. George never understood his English-speaking bride nor her arrogant family, and neither did she understand her Afrikaans husband's rural farm background.

From the first month, the marriage was a kind of comedy of misunderstandings, but it wasn't until seven years later that George met Griet and realized that there might be an alternative. They became good friends while he was an unhappy married man and slept together for the first time shortly after he became an unhappy divorced man.

It was fitting, Griet thought years later, that it should have been seven years. Almost as though he'd worked it out logically. A good average for a relationship. Even the Bible says seven fat years follow seven lean years.

The first year, George marvelled at Griet. He was like an old-fashioned gentleman who'd caught an exotic butterfly in his net. He wanted to pin her down in a display case and study her for the rest of his life. He invited her to come to the cinema with him and spent the whole two hours staring at her profile instead of the film. He never got tired of looking at her.

Griet felt trapped and went out with other men – but returned to the waiting net time and time again. Of her own free will, and subsequently even eagerly. If you have sufficient patience, she thought years later, you can transform almost any animal into a pet.

But if you want to teach a pet to eat out of your hand, both must know who's boss and who's the possessed. George and Griet confused the roles from the beginning. George wanted a pet who'd stimulate him intellectually and sexually. Griet wanted the same thing. Neither of them was prepared to take the responsibility of a proprietor.

When the princess asked the shepherd's clever son how much time made up eternity, he answered, 'A long way from here lies a diamond mountain, one hour high, one hour wide and one hour long, and once each century a bird comes to sharpen its beak on the mountain. Once the whole mountain has been rubbed away, the first second of eternity will have passed.'

The princess was so impressed by the shepherd's son's answers that she decided to marry him. But princesses don't usually make good housewives, and this one didn't know how to use an oven. She put her head in there and spoke the secrets of her heart out loud because she thought no one would be able to hear her.

She didn't know how to use a broom either. She soon learnt, however, that there were ways she hadn't dreamt of, and she began to fly at night.

She began to write at night.

Griet lay on Louise's bed and wondered why it had taken so many months to start understanding why she and her husband had made each other so unhappy. She was naked because Adam had taught her to sleep without clothes again, but tonight she wasn't thinking about sex. She turned over on to her back and wondered if she'd ever see her house again. She linked her hands behind her head in the hollow of her neck and wondered why Louise's flat made her feel like a stranger in her own life.

She closed her eyes in the pitch-dark bedroom and listened to the wind howling at the window. She wished her husband were here to answer her questions. She wished she could feel his thin body against hers just for one last time.

St George, the patron saint of England, had killed a dragon with his sword. St Margaret, the apogee of female purity, put a dragon to flight with her cross. 'Anything You Can Do, I Can Do Better' was the theme song of their namesakes' marriage.

The wind had blown all day as it could only blow in this city. By dusk the trees looked as exhausted as the people, but the onslaught continued. And now, in the silence of the small hours, the wind wailed like a siren. Unmuffled by any traffic noises. Exacerbated by a moonless blackness.

George had become increasingly distanced from his family, seeing less and less of his father and brothers, especially after his mother's death. The opposite had happened to Griet. During her melodramatic teenage years there'd been such a great distance between her and her parents that she felt as though she came from another planet, but now they grew increasingly closer. Maybe she'd grown more tolerant than she'd been in the days of Ziggy Stardust and the Spiders from Mars. Maybe she'd simply learnt to accept her family's faults.

It was easier, in any event, than accepting her own faults.

She wished her ribcage was empty. A great black hole that she could pour all her feelings into so that she'd never be hurt again. Why did she still hope to hear from Adam?

Among the early cynics there had been a woman, Griet had read in surprise in one of her husband's books. There was Antisthenes who started it all, Diogenes who apparently lived in a bath tub, Menedemos the Mad, Krates and his wife, Hipparchia . . .

Why couldn't she stop believing in a god?

'What is God?' Hiero asked the poet Simonides. The poet asked for a day to think it over. The next day he asked for another two days' grace. And from then on he doubled the number of days each time, until he had to tell Hiero at last, 'The longer I think about it, the further I seem to be from any answer.'

'Are you happily married?' Griet had asked her sister Petra the previous evening.

'Yes,' Petra answered without hesitation. 'I'm still not as unhappy with him as I am without him.'

'Is that your definition of a happy relationship?'

'Do you have a better suggestion?'

It was one of those moments of honesty that sometimes catches you unawares in a dark car. They were on their way home after seeing a film that was supposed to be erotic. The two young actresses had frequently stripped to the bone, and the camera, with the practised eye of a voyeur, had fastened itself on the fecund triangle described by nipples and pubic hair. The male lead kept his underpants on, even during the sexual act. ('Boxer shorts,' Petra whispered approvingly.) His genitals, as usual in films like this, were as invisible as the Holy Grail.

'Don't you miss him?' asked Griet. 'You've been here nearly a month now.'

'Not really. It's wonderful to get away once in a while. And when we get together again, there'll be a couple of days of moonlight and roses before the bickering starts up again.'

'What do you bicker about?'

'About his smoking in the bedroom ... about my buying too many groceries in one go and then letting half the things rot in the fridge ... about his splashing water all over the bathroom floor when he bathes ... Oh, you know: the usual things.'

'No, I don't know,' sighed Griet. 'George and I fought because I read the wrong philosophy books and didn't ask enough questions. Or because he never read anything that I wrote.'

'How can you write if you don't understand the world?' George accused her.

'How can I understand the world if I don't write?' was her defence.

'The only way to grow in wisdom is to ask questions,' George told her.

'Writing is also a way of asking questions,' said Griet. 'Don't stories always ask other questions?'

What happened to Gretel after she and Hansel climbed on the goose's back? When they got home to their father? When they grew up?

If all storytellers had to wait until they achieved wisdom, thought Griet in the darkness of her friend's bed, we'd live in a world without stories.

Perhaps in the long run that was the greatest difference between her and her husband, the difference between Simonides and the shepherd's clever son. Simonides was a philosophical poet. The shepherd's clever son was a poetic philosopher.

Why did her husband, who didn't believe in gods or devils or saints or dragons, give his children the names of angels?

23

The Queen on the Pyre

FAR BELOW her, yachts lay on the sea like crumbs on a blue sheet. Before her, on the twentieth floor of her attorney's ivory tower, the air, in a paler shade of blue, also reminded her of a sheet. A faded sheet.

The distant island hung hazily above the water, a flying saucer slowly ascending. If wishes could still come true, Griet speculated, the prisoners would have made that happen long ago. '*The greatest escape*', the newspapers would dub it, a bunch of prisoners escaping miraculously with a whole island. Somewhere over the sea the warders and their families would get the chance to jump off, close enough to be able to swim safely to shore. The island would rise higher and higher and then orbit the earth like a satellite, accompanied by angels and witches and geese and winged horses and exotic nightbirds and other apparitions. And only once the fairy land was liberated from maniac rulers would the island splash down again in the sea near its continent.

'I dreamt about my ex-husband', Griet wrote the night before in her notebook. Then she drew a line through the sentence and wrote: Griet dreamt about her husband.

Make yourself into a fictional character, her shrink had advised her.

*

They stood in a long empty passage in a huge empty building. He told her he was going away and she must take care of the place. She could do whatever she liked, he told her, but she mustn't open the thirteenth door. After he'd left, she opened a door each day. Behind every door there was a bedroom that she recognized immediately.

The room she and Petra had shared as children, the pink-painted wall rough under her fingers when she ran her hand over it in the dark as she told Petra stories. The hostel dormitory she'd hated so much during high school, a grey Cape Education Department blanket as scratchy as steel-wool on a high iron bedstead. The ramshackle outside room full of posters of surfers, where, as a student, she'd first made acquaintance with sex. The one-star hotel room somewhere in the Karoo where she and her husband had passed a sleepless night *en route* to his mother's funeral. She too hot to sleep and he too sad. She lay waiting for him to tell her how he felt, but he didn't say a word all night. The five-star hotel room with the equally strange king-size bed where they woke, both equally alienated, the morning after their wedding.

When she came to the thirteenth door, she couldn't stop herself. She pushed the door open carefully, just a crack, then quickly shut her eyes as a blinding light shone on her. She slammed the door shut, but it was too late. She began to fall, tumbling, and the further she fell the darker everything grew around her.

'Does that mean everything could be over within two weeks?' she asked Hilton Dennis who was fiddling with his tie incessantly today. 'That I could be legally divorced?'

'It's possible.' It was a hand-painted floral silk tie, just a bit too flamboyant in this elegant office. 'If both parties are willing to settle.'

Griet was so relieved she felt she could rise up with the island.

'So, whatever the result of the Rule Forty-five application —'

'Rule Forty-three,' he corrected her irritably.

177

'– Rule Forty-three application is, we can deal with the divorce on the same day?'

'First they get a fright, then they settle.' He smoothed the thinning hair over his forehead and tugged at his collar as though it were too tight. 'That's what I always say.'

He was trying to sound as confident as usual, but his sentences somehow shattered on his glass-topped desk. Maybe he'd had a difficult client. Or lost a case. She actually preferred him this way, Griet decided. A Napoleon who sounded as though he'd at least heard of Waterloo.

Once upon a time, she wrote as a result of her dream, long ago, when wishes still came true, there was a girl who lived in heaven and played with the angels. But because she didn't listen to her master and opened a forbidden door, she fell to earth. She woke up to find herself alone in a wilderness. She wanted to call for help, but she couldn't utter a sound. She'd lost her voice – but she discovered that she could write.

During the years she wandered in the wilderness, she slept at night in the branches of a tree and during the day she sat in its shade and wrote stories in the sand. She didn't know where she'd learnt to write; when she woke up on earth, she could do it.

After many years a prince rode through the wilderness on a green horse. He was so surprised to see the dumb girl with the dirty, hairy body that he tied her to his horse and led her to his kingdom. In his castle he had her washed and shaved and then decided to marry her. She wasn't really beautiful but at least she wouldn't talk the ears off his head like all the beautiful princesses he'd considered.

'Is there any chance of getting it over with sooner?' she wanted to know.

'Why are you in such a hurry?'

How did she explain to her arrogant attorney that she felt like a piece that didn't fit into any jigsaw puzzle? Ill at ease with half her friends who had husbands and children, and equally ill at ease with the other half who had neither. She had a husband, but she had to live alone. She had a child, but he could only live in her heart.

'I feel as though someone's pushed the Pause knob in my life and I've been paused to death. Anything would be preferable to standing still like this. Fast Forward, Play, even Rewind!'

'If you're prepared to give in now . . .'

'I'm prepared to do anything,' she said quickly. 'He can keep the washing machine, the tumbledrier and everything else. I just want to get it over with.'

'I understand how you feel,' soothed her attorney. 'I know you want to get on with your life.'

He's lying, thought Griet, he doesn't know what I'm talking about. He's a general who's enjoying the war. It's an opportunity for him to put his theories and tactics to the test.

But she knew how the soldiers in the trenches felt. She was the one who could lose her head.

'But it would be stupid to withdraw now,' said Hilton Dennis with all the sympathy he could muster. 'You've made it through to the final dress rehearsal. The only thing that remains is the opening night.'

So he saw it as a concert, she thought gloomily. It wasn't even serious enough to be regarded as a war. She was an actress with stage fright, he an impresario with an eye to his bank balance. The longer the show ran, the more money he could make.

'Look, if you're determined to settle, we can do it on the day of the Rule Forty-three decision. We get the chance to negotiate with the other side before we go into court. You can't lose anything by waiting another fortnight.'

'Nothing but a little more self-respect.'

The prince married the dumb girl and became king, and a year later the queen had a baby. The night after the birth, one of the queen's old playmates from heaven appeared and said, 'If you admit that you opened the forbidden door, you'll get your voice back and you'll never have to write again. If you refuse, I'll take your child away with me.'

'But I like writing,' the queen wanted to cry, but she couldn't utter a word. The angel picked up the child and flew away. The next morning, when word got out that the king's child had disappeared without a trace, the people began to whisper that the queen was a cannibal who'd devoured her own offspring.

A year later the dumb queen had another baby. The night after the birth an angel appeared again with the same message as the first time. The queen dissolved in tears and wanted to beg the angel not to take her second child too, but she couldn't utter a word. The angel flew off with her second child, and next morning the rumour spread throughout the kingdom that the queen had devoured her second offspring.

A year later the dumb queen had a third baby. The next night an angel appeared again with the same message as before. The queen fell to her knees before the angel. 'I'll do anything not to lose this third child too!' she wanted to scream, but because she still wouldn't admit that she'd opened the forbidden door, she still couldn't utter a word. And the angel flew off with the third child.

Griet took a packet of cigarettes out of her bag. Her attorney hadn't had a cigarette since she'd arrived fifteen minutes ago, she realized. The big black ashtray, which normally looked like an obscene offering to the god of lung cancer by this time of the day, stood gleaming and empty on the glass-topped desk. Griet experienced a feeling of impending doom, but offered him a cigarette all the same.

'I've given up.' He folded his hands over each other hastily as though they might reach out automatically for the sin before him. He'd never looked so vulnerable. 'I'm trying to give up.'

Now it really was only her and the chap in the Camel ad who still smoked, Griet thought despondently.

'How on earth are you doing that?'

'Doctor's orders.' Griet shoved the cigarettes back in her bag. You can't eat ice cream in front of a hunger-striker. 'But I don't mind if you smoke. Please go ahead.'

He didn't sound very convincing. He hadn't reached the sanctified stage, the stage when Reborn Non-Smokers watch you consume one cigarette after another with a kind of sadistic pleasure. They'll even keep cigarettes in the house just to show you how much will power they have. But her poor attorney was still struggling through purgatory.

'I suppose I could wait another two weeks,' she sighed.

'Of course you can. And you've got a better place to stay now. Why don't you just sit back and relax?'

Only a man could say something like that.

'I can't relax, I have to pack!'

He probably had a wife who packed his bags every time he went off on a business trip.

It wasn't only the packing that made it impossible for her to relax. It was all the forms she had to fill in and all the calls she had to make to let the world know she had a new address.

There were forms for her current account with one bank and her credit card account with another bank; for her personal insurance and her life insurance and her medical aid; for her membership of the Writers' Guild and the Children's Book Forum and the Theatre Club and the Friends of the National Gallery and the AA (the one for motorists, praise be, not the one for alcoholics); for the street children's night shelter and a home for dying cancer sufferers and a crèche in Nyanga; for READ and the Peninsula School Feeding Scheme and the SPCA . . .

If you no longer gave a tenth of your income to the church, you had to get it to the underprivileged some other way.

And then there were all her personal priests who had to know where she was going to be living. Her doctor and her gynaecologist and her dentist and her auditor and her attorney and her analyst. When had her life become so complicated?

Long, long ago, her most important possessions had been a rucksack and a pair of hiking boots. She'd toured Europe, without credit cards, without personal insurance, without an attorney. She'd slept on trains and at stations. She'd been fearless and happy. She hadn't needed a therapist.

She'd never be that happy again, even if she sold all her possessions tomorrow, consigned all her personal priests to hell, and tore up all her membership cards and insurance policies.

She couldn't travel in Europe with a backpack again; she'd never be able to find one big enough for all her neuroses.

And she couldn't sell her sadness along with all her other possessions.

'Why don't you take a few days off work?' The change in her attorney's voice told her that her time with him was up. 'To settle down in your new flat?'

He tugged at his collar again and swivelled his neck like a dog that's trying to get out of a leash. The poor fellow had put on weight, like everyone who gives up smoking, and his wife hadn't bought him new shirts yet.

'I don't have any more leave due to me.' With her wretched pregnancies and all her crises she'd used up her quota. 'And I can't afford to take unpaid leave.'

'Never mind, in two weeks' time you'll be able to afford a holiday,' promised Hilton Dennis and stood up to see her out of his office.

And so my story's almost done, thought Griet.

The next day all the people rose up against the queen who'd devoured her children. The people demanded that she be burnt to death. The king shrugged and rode off on his green horse. The queen was dragged to the pyre by her hair. As the flames started to lick at her feet, she found her voice and screamed, 'I opened the forbidden door!'

And it grew dark suddenly and the clouds were ripped asunder. Rain drenched the earth and quenched the fire. And when it grew light again, the queen was gone. She had disappeared without trace, just like her children.

She apparently became a saint who killed dragons. She was seen at a festival of witches in England. She was seen on a beach in South America – riding a green horse. She changed her name and became a writer. No one will ever know what really happened.

24

The Devil Takes Care of His Sister

'*SO, WHAT DO* you think of her?' asked Tienie. They were in Griet's new flat.

'Well, she looks . . .' What do you say about someone you've scarcely spoken to? wondered Griet helplessly. Someone who isn't particularly large or small or pretty or ugly. Someone who doesn't have any noticeable physical characteristic – like a long nose, green eyes or a sensual mouth – that you could remark on. 'She looks . . . nice.' She laughed at her own clumsiness.

'Exactly what Ma said! Anyone who dresses more conservatively than Nella – and that's ninety-nine per cent of the human race – is classified as "nice" these days. I really miss the good old days when I could still shock my family.'

Tienie followed her into the living room where she was arranging her books.

'I'm glad you took your friend home and introduced her. I was beginning to suspect you were ashamed of your family.'

'My God, Griet, you sound more like Ma every day. My relationships are usually over so quickly that it's not worth the trouble of involving the family.'

'Well, this one's already lasted an entire holiday.'

'Don't say it out loud,' whispered Tienie. 'In case fate overhears you.'

Griet sat on the floor among the piles of boxes. Her hair was bundled up under a bandanna and her face was streaked with grime. But when she moved in here next week, her books would be unpacked to help her feel at home.

'Ma had a word with me after you and Elsie left,' said Griet without looking at her sister.

'What did she say?'

Tienie sat down gingerly on a box of books. Griet lit a cigarette and inhaled deeply while she wondered how to broach the subject diplomatically.

'Ma knows you're gay, Tienie. Why don't you talk about it to her?'

Tienie looked down at her hands without saying anything.

'I know you're going to say I don't know what I'm talking about and Ma would never understand.'

'More or less.' Tienie smiled.

'Maybe she won't understand.' Griet stared at the cigarette in her grimy hand. 'But she wants you to be honest with each other.'

'Did she say that?'

Not in so many words, thought Griet.

'Is she happy?' Gretha wanted to know.

'Well, she probably doesn't wake up every morning with a song on her lips, Ma.'

'I don't either,' sighed Gretha. 'That's not what I'm asking.'

Griet and her mother sat at the kitchen table having a last cup of coffee the night Tienie and her lover had come to supper. Gretha leant with an elbow on the table, fingering the soft skin under her eyes. Without any make-up she looked older than usual.

'Is she so convinced of her . . .' Gretha looked at her daughter helplessly. 'Is she certain that she can't find a man who'll make her happy?'

Poor Rapunzel, thought Griet. One of her daughters became a lesbian, another dressed like a clown. Her first-born lost her husband, her house, her children and stepchildren and tried to climb into an oven. Her only decent daughter lived light years away in another country. Her only son refused to play either the hero or the martyr and ran away from the army. Her life really hadn't followed the path she'd dreamt of long ago in her tower.

'Have you ever discussed it with Pa?' she asked her mother.

'What?'

'The fact that he'll never be called upon to propose a toast at Tienie's wedding.'

'There are things you discuss with your husband, Gretel, and there are things you don't discuss with your husband.'

'She wants you to be happy,' Griet told Tienie.

'And happiness means getting married and having children?' Tienie's heavy eyebrows drew together, a black curtain over her eyes. 'It's those fairy tales of yours that have fucked the world up, Griet, do you realize that?'

Griet knew when not to fight with her bedevilled sister.

'Every fairy tale that Ma ever read to us ended in marriage.'

'Not *Hansel and Gretel*,' Griet countered.

'Why isn't it called *Gretel and Hansel*? If Gretel was the heroine, shouldn't her name be mentioned first?'

'Would you prefer to have grown up without fairy tales?'

'No,' said Tienie, still scowling. 'It probably wouldn't have helped, they've got so many other ways of getting the message across. But don't you think new fairy tales should be spun for a new world?'

'That's what I'm doing,' sighed Griet. 'I've published a book of modern fairy stories, but not one of you has read it yet, because you think fairy stories are for children.'

'Will you lend it to me?' asked Tienie, laughing at Griet's obvious pleasure. 'I promise I'll read it.'

Noddy comes in from the cold [wrote Louise

from a frozen Britain]. The BBC is apparently going to make a 'new' version of the Toytown saga. The golliwogs have been thrown out in case their presence is seen as racist; Noddy doesn't sleep with Big Ears any more in case that's seen as a case of you-know-what; Miss Rap will become Miss Prim(!), Mister Plod the Policeman has been forbidden to spank and – wait for this – Martha the Monkey presents a strong role-model for women.

Sometimes I wonder about this world we live in.

As I sit here under three blankets writing this, BBC2 is showing a documentary on over-population, pollution, famine, drought and babies dying by the million of diarrhoea. Doom, Death and Destruction. And I worry that I'm eating too much chocolate. Makes you drink, doesn't it?

Isn't it better to live a completely decadent life? To eat and drink and fornicate to your heart's content? And then to die while there's still an earth to die on?

Late last night I caught the end of one of those depressing black and white movies – I don't know what the name was, but they should issue a warning over the screen when they show stuff like that: 'This might be damaging to your mental health' or something. The woman's husband, her housekeeper and her friend have already left her by the time I began watching, and then she gets a telegram with the news of her sister's death. And then it ends, and the last words on the screen are: 'People who live unto themselves are left unto themselves.'

'Alternative fairy tales have been around for centuries,' said Griet, opening the box she'd packed her fairy-tale collections into. 'But they never became as well known as the safe ones and the proper ones that asked the right questions. One of my favourites is about a soldier who served in hell for seven years. The devil taught him how to make music and gave him a big sack of gold, and then he travelled the world as a musician and ended up marrying the daughter of a king. What's the moral of a story like that?'

'It's OK to work for the devil?'

'The devil looks after his own?'

'Have you heard from your angelic visitor again?'

'No,' sighed Griet, 'and I doubt that I ever will. And I can't understand why I feel so bloody disappointed about it! It's probably just my ego – can't bear to be forgotten, not by George, not by Adam . . .'

Tienie looked at her silently, like her therapist. Thank heaven she didn't have a file on her knee.

Angelici, Griet had learnt recently, were heretics who advocated the worship of angels.

'Do you know what I want?' she asked her clever sister. 'I want someone to fall in love with me again. Or doesn't it happen any more after thirty? I know, one day when I'm in an old people's home, the senile old codger in the room next door will be smitten. If I ever reach the age when you're allowed into an old people's home. If I don't die of disappointment along the way because I'm no longer the *femme fatale* I was at twenty.'

Angels are divided into nine orders and the nine orders into three circles – from seraphim and cherubim in the lowest circles to archangels and angels in the very highest. And her Angel Gabriel was no cherub, she thought sadly.

'I know I'll fall in love again. I'll carry on being idiotic until the day I die – "and then probably fuck that up too". If only it was possible to fall in love without getting hurt. I've had a gutful of getting hurt.'

'You'll keep on,' said Tienie. 'It's in your blood. We've got the same blood.'

'I had an Aids test today.' When Griet saw the surprise on her sister's face, she lit another cigarette immediately. 'I've been putting it off for months. The older I get the more cowardly I become.'

'No.' Her clever sister shook her head. 'We get braver as we get older. The older we get, the more courage we need just to get up in the morning. We don't leap off cliffs as we used to as children, but we have to make an enormous leap of faith each day just to stay alive.'

'Well, I took a massive leap over my own fears today,' said Griet.

She thought her GP would be shocked when she said she wanted to be tested for Aids. And then she was the one who was shocked speechless: he suggested she have a syphilis test at the same time.

'Syphilis?' She swallowed hard, her mouth dry from surprise. 'But I have only had . . . only slept with one man since . . . since I've been on my own.'

'Of course,' said her middle-aged doctor with a soothing smile. 'But there's always the chance that you might sleep with someone else, isn't there? Unless you're getting married in the next few days?'

She gazed at her doctor's silver-grey hair and his silver-framed spectacles. He was the sort of man who'd even pronounce a death sentence as a rhetorical question, she thought. 'You have only three days left to live, you know?'

He sent her, form in hand, to the pathologists' laboratory three floors down in the same building. She gave the forms to a virginal girl behind a counter, one who'd surely never needed to be tested for any venereal disease. She smiled at Griet and sent her to a room about the size of a reasonably big fridge. Another virgin came in and fastened a blood-pressure band around her upper arm. Maybe they all looked like virgins to her because she felt like a syphilitic old slut.

She was still trying to think of something witty to say — if all else fails, laugh — but then her blood samples had already been taken and it was all over. All but the results which she would only have after the weekend. Because she'd been stupid enough to have the test done on a Friday, she had to live through the entire weekend with the nightmare of a venereal disease. Two frightful venereal diseases. Three long nights to lie awake through.

'Aha, here it is,' she said, hauling out the book of fairy stories.

As she passed it to her sister, a card fell out of it. Griet picked it up, surprised because it looked so unfamiliar. On the outside there was a picture of a man and a woman on two striped merry-go-round horses. The background was blood red. She opened it. '*My dearest George, I hope we stay on the merry-go-round for ever and ever. Love, Griet.*' The date was his birthday last year.

Three months before she moved out. She sat and stared at the words until they started to slide off the card. Her tears were making the ink run, she realized. She'd been fighting the tears for months – and here she was dissolving over sixteen words in her own handwriting.

'Are you OK?' Tienie's voice came from a long way off.

'No.'

She dropped her head into her hands and her shoulders started to shake. She was crying, she thought in wonderment, over a silly little birthday greeting.

25

Rose-Red Loses Her Man

'*LET'S DRINK* to my last night with the cockroaches.' Griet lifted her glass high like a freedom fist. 'And to whatever awaits me in the new flat.'

'*Viva,*' said Jans, clinking his glass against hers. 'May the gods be good to you.'

'I'm sure they will be,' said Griet recklessly. 'They owe me a favour after the last year.'

Don't tempt fate, she heard her grandfather's guardian angel whisper in her ear. But her father's voice was louder than any angel's. Be positive, he said, as always, and for once she wanted to be an obedient daughter. She and Jans were sitting on the balcony of Louise's flat, she on the only chair and he on her packed suitcase.

'When is D-Day?'

Jans was wearing his white attorney's shirt. His collar was unbuttoned and his striped tie hung loose. A film of perspiration gleamed on his upper lip.

'D for Divorce?' Griet was also still in her office clothes, but she'd kicked her shoes off and her feet were propped on the railing. 'Hopefully next week.'

The sun was setting after an oppressive summer's day and the light was fading faster and faster. Tomorrow marked the beginning of a new month, she thought gratefully, the second month of a new year. Tomorrow night she'd sleep for the first time in her new flat. She didn't have a bed or a fridge or a stove or even a bookcase, but she felt that she could get by with nothing but hope. Maybe even without cigarettes and a shrink, she tried to convince herself.

She'd told Rhonda that afternoon that she wanted to come only once a month from now on.

'If you feel it'll be enough, Griet.' Rhonda folded her hands on her lap, gold bracelet on the right wrist, gold Rolex on the other. 'But don't hesitate to ring if you change your mind.'

'I won't.'

She wouldn't change her mind, she decided.

'How are you getting on with the fairy story?'

'I don't know whether it's still a fairy story. I don't know what it is any more. But I'm writing like never before.'

'About your grandparents?'

'More about myself,' she said apologetically.

'It's time, Griet.' Rhonda leant forward slightly on the red sofa. Griet cast a quick glance at the clock on the wall. Her hour couldn't be up already. 'It's high time that you stopped running away.'

Griet folded her hands on her lap too. Her arms were bare and her nails were grubby.

Didn't her shrink know that you could become airborne if you ran fast enough for long enough?

'I'll get the food from the oven,' said Jans, getting up from the case with a groan. He'd picked up chop suey and spring rolls from a Chinese take-away on his way over. He pushed her back into her chair when she got up to help. 'More wine?'

'You're my hero.' Griet laughed, curling her toes over the railing and raising her arms high above her head. 'What would I do without you?'

He looked down at her, his head tilted slightly, his expression unfathomable.

'You'd probably survive,' he said as he walked away.

She'd known him for a decade, she realized as she watched him go. She'd seen him naked, she'd seen him drunk, she'd seen him in love – often. But she'd never realized before what a sexy bum he had. Griet cast her eyes up to heaven and decided it was the new moon that was affecting her hormones. It wasn't called the witching moon for nothing.

'Let's drink to Hansel and the witch,' said Jans when he came back with the food and wine on a tray. 'And to Mandela who is to be released one of these days.'

Far below them the city lights started to flicker like candles in a cathedral. This was the last time that she'd see the world from this borrowed balcony. Venus twinkled in the sky high above the highest building, a brooch pinned to the darkening air.

'We should drink to Gwen,' she remembered suddenly. 'I heard yesterday that she's pregnant.'

'What?' Jans almost lost his balance on the suitcase. 'What's Klaus got to say about it?'

'He doesn't know yet. She moved out. And she doesn't know whether she wants to go back to him.'

Gwen had still been in shock when she met Griet for lunch the day before.

'I can't understand how it happened,' she'd mumbled over and over again. 'I just can't understand it.'

'Immaculate conception?' Griet suggested at last, weary of the garbled babbling.

'I threw out the Pill months ago in the hope that something would happen. I'd begun to accept that I was barren.'

Gwen stared at the glass of healthsome orange juice that Griet had ordered for her.

'You'll have to cut out all that coffee.' Griet didn't smoke a single cigarette during the meal. She could do anything for unborn babies. Her heart was aching with joy for her friend, and with longing for a child of her own. 'Ask me. I know all about pregnancy.'

Gwen burst out laughing when the waitress put two bowls of Greek salad and a little basket of wholewheat rolls on the table.

'I wanted cheesecake and coffee, Griet!'

'You'll have to start eating more healthily.'

'Anyway, as I was saying, things between Klaus and me got so tense that in the end I had no choice but to move out. It's up to him whether he wants to spend the rest of his life sitting beside his ex-wife in a shrink's office discussing his delinquent son's problems, or whether he wants to live with me and face up to *our* problems. And three days after I move out, I discover I'm pregnant!'

'And now?'

'I don't know. I don't want to go back to him just because I'm going to have a baby. We're too old for a shotgun wedding. Aren't we? What do you think?'

She already looked pregnant. Not radiantly pregnant as the women's magazines always put it, but rather confusedly pregnant. Her skin seemed smoother. Of course, that could also be nothing more than her own over-active imagination, Griet told herself. Just the word pregnant was apparently enough to send her intelligence flying out through her ears.

'How far gone are you?'

'Already nearly ten weeks. I thought it must be early menopause when I didn't menstruate.'

'Do you think you're going to be able to go it alone, Gwen?' she asked carefully, like her therapist.

Gwen stared at her orange juice for a long time and then smiled. 'Would you mind holding my hand in the labour ward, Griet?'

'He'll want to have a say about the child,' said Jans beside her on the balcony.

'Men always want to have a say about what becomes of their semen.' Griet struggled to get the chop suey to her mouth with the chopsticks: she was determined not to resort to knife and fork. 'They should just be a bit more careful before spewing it out all over the place.'

I'm dreaming about Chinese food and sex [wrote a still-yearning Louise from London]. It's got so bad that I phoned Rony in Hong Kong before dawn yesterday. I told him I was afraid we wouldn't recognize each other and couldn't he please send me a photograph. Then I'd send him one of me. (I'll show you mine if you show me yours.) Now I know how someone feels who writes to a Lonely Hearts Club. You have to be fucking lonely to phone Hong Kong at five on a Thursday morning.

But the oddest thing of all is that for the first time in months I've started treating my husband decently. I realize I'm over-reacting, as usual, but I feel like a person again – not just an unhappy wife. And God knows, Griet, if it takes an affair to make married life bearable, then it was worth the trouble of ringing Hong Kong. Even though my husband will probably throw me out of the house when the phone bill comes.

'Talking of sex, I read a report that'll interest you.'

Griet imagined she could hear Jans smile beside her. She gave the chopsticks a break.

'Do you know what *koro* is?' Jans said.

She had no idea what to expect.

'It's Malay for tortoise head – and the poetic medical term for Penile Shrinkage Syndrome.'

'For *what*?'

'Penile . . .'

'I heard what you said, Jans.' Griet laughed. She'd thought it was a condition that only existed in her imagination. Something caused by castrating witches. *That shrinking feeling.*

'It's apparently fairly common in the East. The sufferer grabs his penis before it disappears altogether, to prevent himself from turning into a ghost. The anxiety attack can last for up to two days.'

'Why a ghost?'

'Ghosts don't have sexual organs.'

'Don't they?'

'Can you imagine a ghost with an erection?'

Griet shook her head and looked at the mountain that was flaunting itself under the floodlights like a prima donna. She was going to miss this view, she realized for the first time. Tomorrow she started all over again, she told herself. Scarlett O'Hara in *Gone with the Wind*. She raised her glass to her therapist who was flying over the crescent moon on a broomstick, her hair blown every which way, her head thrown back like that time when she had laughed in her consulting room. It was a night when anything was possible.

26

The Gooseherd Goes Hunting

ONCE UPON a time a bald king decided to ban all colours except orange, white and blue. Any other colour gave him a headache. Red made him think of Communists and Other Instigators (Banned), green made him think of Marijuana (Forbidden), purple of Alternative Newspapers (Forbidden), yellow of Chinese Communists and Other Instigators (Banned), brown of District Six (Destroyed) and black, the wickedest of all colours, of the Unthinkable Future. The Future he'd like to Forbid, Ban and Destroy.

It was naturally not child's play to get rid of colours, but the bald king spared neither money nor effort. All trees, shrubs and plants were weeded out, except for the few that bore only orange flowers and fruit. The strelitzia was instated as the new national flower and the queen wore one pinned to her shoulder. The marigold was worn by the king in his buttonhole. Oranges, mandarins, pawpaws, melons, carrots and pumpkin were the only fruit and vegetables allowed. All buildings were painted in the desirable colours, all traffic lights were altered so from then on they showed blue, orange and white lights, and all streets were surfaced with white cement in place of black tar. Fortunately the sea, the sky and the mountains were blue, and the clouds and the beaches white, otherwise the king would never have been able to get rid of his headache.

But then something very odd happened, even for a fairy tale. The bald king was declared crazy by his own wise men and councillors. A new bald king ascended the throne and astounded everyone by inviting all the colours back again. Even the most dangerous of all combinations, the three colours which had always made the previous king's index finger stand straight up in the air with fear and rage. The black, green and yellow of the Unthinkable Future.

The world rejoiced and even the angels were amazed. The people were overjoyed because they could once again drink ruby red wine instead of carrot juice and they could pelt each other with rotten tomatoes instead of oranges. The trees and shrubs and other plants grew again, and for the first time the grass was just as green on both sides of the fence.

'I know I said I wouldn't be back for a month,' Griet told Rhonda, twirling a strand of hair faster and faster round her finger. 'But I didn't know the ANC was going to be unbanned and Nelson Mandela was going to be released and the exiles were going to come back. I didn't know everything was going to change so fast. And not just here, the whole world! The Berlin Wall pulled down and that Rumanian dictator shot dead on Christmas Day – couldn't they have waited one more day? – and the whole of Eastern Europe imploding and God only knows what's happening with Communism.'

'And you feel anxious.'

'Anxious!' If her finger wound any faster she was going to take off like a helicopter. 'I've lived all my life in a world where everything was as predictable as . . . as . . . as your facial expressions! And now everything's changing overnight, everything in my personal life and everything around me. Of course I feel anxious.'

The faintest shadow of a smile hovered fleetingly at the corners of her therapist's mouth. Rhonda did have a sense of humour after all, Griet decided. But she tried just as hard to keep it a secret as Grandma Lina had tried to hide her tree-climbing.

'Is the whole world going to be transformed into a capitalistic heaven?' Reflected light flashed blindingly off the face of Rhonda's Rolex as she wrote something on her lap. It was a long time since she'd last written something in that file, Griet realized, but nothing could get her into more of a state today than she was already. 'One great big Hollywood where the rich get even richer and the poor even poorer?'

'It's understandable that you should feel insecure now, Griet.'

'I don't give a fuck about whether it's understandable or not, I just want to be in control again!'

'Of what, Griet?'

'Of my emotions,' Griet answered slowly. 'Of what I write. Of my own little world.'

Rhonda nodded rhythmically with every word.

'I lost my husband, I lost my house, I lost my children and my stepchildren. One of my sisters has gone back to Johannesburg and my other sister leaves for New York next week and my lover is back in London. My mother and father are growing older and dying. I am growing older and dying. All I have left to lose is my mind.'

'You were legally divorced last week, Griet,' soothed her therapist. 'I expected to hear from you. I would have been surprised if you hadn't phoned.'

She looked like the ventriloquist's doll that Griet had seen on television the week before. The lips moved and the voice created an illusion of life, but the face remained a doll's face.

She was legally divorced. She sat in her advocate's office while her advocate and her attorney negotiated with the advocate and attorney who had been employed by her husband. Her ex-husband. She smoked all of her only packet of cigarettes in three hours. And then she was seized by panic. Since her little Napoleon of an attorney was still waging his war on nicotine, he couldn't help her either. In the end, out of sheer desperation, she sent a messenger to the enemy camp's waiting room to beg a cigarette from George. If she couldn't get a damages deposit from her husband, then at least she could get a cigarette.

She flipped through a pile of magazines, *Time, The Spectator, The Economist*, and read several articles carefully without taking in a single word. She read something about Georges Simenon writing a book in eleven days. It made her feel even worse. She couldn't even *read* a book in eleven days.

But there was one headline that stuck in her whirling brain: '*Renaissance in Witchcraft*'. An unprepossessing little article about a modern witch and her husband. Morgana and Merlin. They offered classes in Wicca (white witchcraft) in a house near London. The classes included the history of witchcraft and 'psychic self-defence'. The latter immediately seized Griet's imagination.

She wondered if she shouldn't write to Louise about the Wicca classes in her vicinity. Maybe they'd distract her attention from Hong Kong and chop suey.

I got a photograph [wrote a slightly calmer Louise from London], and he has got a paunch. And he's bald. So what? I've got a lot of time to think before his conference begins here in London. To dream about Hong Kong and try to accept my husband for what he is. I block my ears when he farts in the shower. I have stopped chucking orange juice at him. If I really can't help myself, I chuck water at him.

'I CAN'T COPE!' she told her analyst.

'The worst is over, Griet.'

'Says who?' Griet grabbed her bag. Her hands trembled as she took out her cigarettes. Was this how it felt to be divorced? 'My friend is pregnant and I'm worried sick about her. She simply accepts that everything will be fine. I can't. I simply cannot accept that a pregnancy will run its course successfully. I can't accept that anything will run its course successfully. Well, I suppose I can believe that it might turn out OK in the end, but only after everything that could go wrong has gone wrong along the way. Is that pessimistic optimism? Or optimistic pessimism?'

'It sounds as though you have plenty of material to write about.'

'If I could only trust my PC. I blinked yesterday and the machine swallowed three thousand words. Just like that. The one day that I don't back up, probably because my spirit was still hanging in the divorce court. What did I expect? Sympathy from a psychopath?'

'*If a machine gets very complicated, it becomes pointless to argue whether it's got a mind of its own*', said a certain Professor Donald Michie of Scotland, according to this morning's paper. '*It so obviously does, that you had better get on good terms with it and shut up about the metaphysics.*'

It had to be Scotland. It just showed you, as Grandpa Kerneels would have said.

The tale of the twelve huntsmen, that was what Griet had typed yesterday on her psychopathic computer. (With commentary from a cynical gooseherd.)

Once upon a time there was a princess whose betrothed had to marry another girl. (Had to marry?) So the princess gathered together eleven ladies-in-waiting and they disguised themselves as huntsmen and rode to the castle of her betrothed. (Aha! Twelve strong roles for women!) He didn't recognize her and took them into his service as huntsmen. (Male Amnesia Syndrome, a well-known medical condition, like *koro*.)

But in the castle there dwelt a magic lion who told the king that his twelve huntsmen were not really twelve huntsmen, but twelve young women. When the king refused to believe him, the lion said he'd prove it if the king would strew peas on the floor the following day. Men walk with a steady tread over peas, said the lion, but women tiptoe so the peas roll about. (Says who?)

But in the castle there was also a good servant who warned the huntsmen that they were to be tested. Be manly, the princess told her ladies-in-waiting, and walk on the peas. (Force yourself, doll.) The next day the young women walked so manfully over the peas that the king decided the lion had been pulling his leg. But the lion had another plan and said the king should have twelve spinning wheels brought out. Men hardly spare a glance for a spinning wheel, said the lion, but no young woman could resist it. (Says who?)

Once again the servant warned the twelve huntsmen and the princess said to her ladies-in-waiting: 'Be manly and ignore the spinning wheels.' (We will live for you, we will die for you, we will never glance at a spinning wheel . . .) The next day they ignored the spinning wheels and the King decided never to believe the lion again. From then on the king took his twelve huntsmen out with him every time he went hunting.

Then came the announcement that the girl he had to marry (had to marry?) was on her way to the castle. The poor princess's heart was breaking and she fell to the ground in a dead faint. (Just shows, she could walk on peas and ignore spinning wheels, but she really couldn't control her own heart.)

That's what Griet typed, and then the story disappeared without trace. Like the dumb queen's children. Her computer was a devourer of stories, Griet decided, who deserved to die on a pyre.

'Has anything good happened?' Rhonda asked eventually.

Griet looked away from her therapist towards Mickey Mouse on the yellow wall, at the yellow and red and blue stripes on the curtains, to the armchair into which the last shreds of her dignity had sunk again today.

'I haven't got Aids,' she answered.

When she rang her doctor to get the results of her Aids test, his receptionist asked her to try again in an hour's time. 'The doctor is very busy this morning.'

'So am I,' Griet protested, 'and I can't wait another hour.'

She'd already waited a whole weekend. Did this receptionist know what it felt like to be tortured for three whole nights by an Aids result? *Of course you haven't got Aids*, she assured herself a thousand times over the weekend. *But what if* . . . the devil whispered every time, and then the angel on her shoulder got such a fright that all she could hear was the fluttering of wings.

'Look,' she said to the receptionist when she rang again an hour later to be told that the doctor was still busy, 'I just want to know the results of a test so that I can get on with my life. I don't have to talk to the doctor. Can't you give me the results?'

'The doctor said he wanted to speak to you himself, Mrs Moore.'

My name is Griet Swart, she wanted to say, but she'd lost her voice. Her doctor wanted to speak to her himself. *That meant she had Aids.*

The next hour she spent in hell. She sat staring at her computer in her office full of children's books while she sold her body to the devil. Syphilis, she said. She'd take syphilis if he took Aids. She'd even settle for lung cancer. Any cancer.

'The result was negative,' she told her analyst. 'When the doctor told me, I nearly collapsed, because negative has always meant bad news to me. Think positive, my father always says. But in this case negative is obviously positive. And positive negative. It just shows you how deceptive language can be.'

It just shows you. Why did her doctor want to talk to her himself? she wanted to know when she found her tongue again. Because it was part of his job, he told her, to convey the results of tests to patients personally. How would she have felt if his receptionist had told her she was HIV positive?

She couldn't imagine that she'd have felt any worse than if her doctor had told her himself.

'I don't know if you want to hear this, Griet, but you are coping.' Rhonda shut the file on her lap and put it on the sofa beside her. The gold pen and gold watch reflected the sunlight together for a moment. She folded her hands on her empty lap.

'Sure. I can cope. I can bang nails into walls and change the batteries in my vibrator myself. I've learnt to use my head like a man and to enjoy my body like a man enjoys his. But what do I do about my heart?'

'Naturally you feel anxious because everything is changing so quickly,' soothed Rhonda. 'We're all in the same boat. But you've come a long way these last few months.'

The longest way in the world, Griet wanted to tell her therapist, is the few metres a frightened woman has to cross between the oven door and the front door.

The king crouched down beside his unconscious huntsman to try and help, Griet typed into her computer once she'd given up all hope of getting the rest of her story back again. When he removed the huntsman's glove, he recognized the ring he'd given to his betrothed. (After a number of hunting expeditions he still didn't recognize her face, but he recognized the ring immediately.) And his heart was so moved (by a ring!) that he sent a messenger to the other girl telling her she should return to her own kingdom (not the sort of news that a decent man would send with a messenger, is it?) because you didn't use a new key if you'd found an old one.

(The moral of the story? A princess who wants to marry a man like this deserves all she gets. Not so?)

27

Scheherazade and the Apple of All Evil

'*IT'S BEEN* an exhausting week,' said Griet, 'and I'm talking only of my own life. Not to mention everything that's going on in the country.'

'Is Jans going to join us tonight?' Gwen was wearing a long dress that would still be loose enough when she was nine months pregnant, even though she didn't even have the suggestion of a stomach yet. 'Or is he working too hard on the New South Africa?'

'Politics are more important than parties, Gwen.' Griet poured soda into a wine glass for her friend. 'But he promised to come by later.'

'What does he say about all the changes?'

'He says the world is experiencing a moment of hope. Like Camelot, or the Renaissance, or the Kennedy years in America. He says in a year or two we'll look back nostalgically to this moment.'

Gwen shook her head and gazed at the bubbles in her soda water. 'It's all too good to keep going for long, isn't it?'

Griet looked round her, at the family and friends she had invited to her new flat tonight. She had taken the first step, she thought gratefully, away from the oven door. She didn't have a stove, but she had bought herself a microwave. So small that even a dwarf couldn't get his head into it. She didn't have a bed to push under her mattress or bookcases for her books. But it could have been worse, as her father would have said. She could have had a bed without a mattress or a bookcase with no books.

'And how was your D-Day?' Gwen wanted to know.

'Just as messy as the one in the Second World War. Napoleon against Churchill. My attorney versus my husband's attorney – my ex-husband's attorney. We will fight them in chambers! We will fight them in court! We will never give up! Or whatever it was that Churchill said.'

'It's one of the few things I haven't experienced,' said Gwen, sounding almost regretful for a moment. 'Is it as bad as they say?'

'Worse. It's absurd. There you sit: you and the man you've lived with – and conceived three children with – for seven years. You sit in separate waiting rooms while a team of attorneys and advocates and advisors negotiate behind closed doors. And all I could think of the whole time were Churchill's war speeches. Never before has so little been done by so many for so few.'

'For so much money?'

'You wait a whole day,' Griet laughed, 'clinging to your sense of humour like a castaway hangs on to a splinter of plank.'

'But in the end you came to some sort of agreement?'

'In the end our legal teams came to some sort of agreement. I felt that I no longer had a say in my own divorce. I just wanted to close my eyes and wake up somewhere else. Even Louise's kitchen was cosy in comparison with that waiting room.'

Gwen stroked her stomach thoughtfully, her eyes on Klaus at the other end of the living room. For the first time since Griet had known her, she looked at home in her own body. The loose dress emphasized her broad hips and large breasts.

'But it looks as though things are going better with you than they are with me?'

'I don't know how long the peace is going to last,

Griet.' Gwen sipped her soda water. 'But everything seems fine right now. Klaus said he wanted to try again – before he knew about the baby.'

'And when he heard the news?'

'Well, even if he'd wanted to, he couldn't very well abscond seconds after declaring his everlasting love. I never thought I'd be grateful that Klaus is German! But you know what Germans are like: soppy about babies and pregnant women.'

'I know,' smiled Griet. 'The Brothers Grimm even believed in happy endings. Are you going to be married?'

'We'll have to see. I don't know, Griet, I'm probably too old or cynical, but I don't want to plan ahead any more. At the moment I just take things day by day.'

She smiled at Griet and moved back to Klaus. He looked down at her, sliding an arm round her hips. Protectively. Possessively? Things might still work out for them, thought Griet. Whatever that meant these days.

'I love your flat,' Nella said from behind Griet. 'It's a vast improvement on Louise's place.'

'A park bench would be an improvement on Louise's place, Nella. I'm so glad you came.'

Nella's purple velvet frock and green velvet hat made her look like a peacock in a pen of doves. Griet thought she'd seen the hat ages ago in her mother's wardrobe. It could also have belonged to one of her grandmothers.

'I notice you don't have any ashtrays in your new life. Are you going to stop smoking at last?'

'No. Yes, of course I'll give up sometime, but not yet. I left all my ashtrays in George's house by accident.'

'I'm never going to give up,' declared Nella, drawing sensually on a long slim cheroot. 'Who wants to grow old?'

'I also said that when I was your age,' sighed Griet. 'You can use a saucer as an ashtray.'

She'd also left her kettle in her old home, and half her towels, and all her pillows. But she'd read somewhere long ago that people who sleep without pillows aren't so prone to getting double chins. And she didn't really need all those towels. And she could boil water in her microwave oven until she got a new kettle. Life was actually simpler than she'd reckoned.

'And if I should grow old against my own better judgement, and get Alzheimer's or just become senile, it's better for my brain to smoke,' said Nella confidently. 'I read that in *GQ*. They did tests on old people and Alzheimer patients and found that smokers perform better – mentally – than non-smokers. And that the improvement was dramatic among Alzheimer sufferers. And the more they smoke, the better they perform.'

'Terrific. So if I don't die of lung cancer or a heart attack or any other condition attached to smoking – or cynicism or any other psychological condition – I can become a thinking senior? Is that what *Gentlemen's Quarterly* claims, Nella?'

'All I'm saying is that there are more arguments in favour of smoking than just being thin and decadent.' Nella let the smoke curl from her nostrils in lazy spirals.

She's so young, thought Griet, she didn't have a single scar on her body or her heart yet.

Petra had just appeared in the doorway. She wore a close-fitting black dress with a plunging neckline, her mouth flashing scarlet as a traffic light. Now we'll see some action, thought Griet when she noticed Anton's reaction to the red light. She wondered if he would tell her sister how erotic she looked when she brushed against tables and chairs. She wondered whether she should warn her sister that he was married to a friend.

'I wonder what Ma would say about Marko's partner,' she said to her youngest sister. 'Why does he always go for girls who look like eleven-year-old orphans?'

'Well . . .' Nella speculated through a cloud of smoke, 'as a little boy he always brought stray dogs and injured birds home.'

'Maybe it's not so bad having a South African passport any more,' Louise had said over the telephone earlier that evening, with more optimism in her voice than Griet had heard for months. The world really was experiencing a moment of hope if even her cynical friend could sound like this. 'Or is that just wishful thinking?'

'Does this mean you're coming home?'

'Don't jump to conclusions.' She hesitated for a second. 'But it makes it easier to cope with Andrew if I know I can come home. And we might even do our great African Safari in a few years, Griet. From Cape Town to Cairo – with South African passports!'

Griet laughed. As long as they'd known each other, they'd dreamt of travelling the length of Africa one day, getting to know their own continent. And it was the first time in months that Louise had referred to her husband by name, she realized.

'And what news from the Far East?' asked Griet.

'I'm still in lust.' Louise's sigh fell heavily between them and subsided slowly into silence. 'Even though he's bald and he has a paunch. I'm everything now that I never wanted to be, you know. Overweight, over thirty and unhappily married – with sexual fantasies about a randy middle-aged Israeli!'

'Welcome to reality, as you told me long ago, my dearest friend!'

'Oh yes, I bumped into Adam in the pub round the corner.' Be still, my heart, thought Griet. 'He couldn't stop talking about you. We spoke in Afrikaans, otherwise the girl with him would have gone green with envy. I don't know what you did to him but he sounds bewitched.'

'What did the girl look like?'

'Do you really want to know?'

'Yes. I can take it. No. Don't tell me. I can guess. Very young, very pretty and very thin.'

'And very stupid,' Louise added. 'He said he'd never met such an exciting woman with such a strong personality as you.'

'Isn't that what they always say? And the next day you wake up alone again.'

'Now you sound almost as cynical as I am, Gretel.' Louise's voice sounded more sad than cynical.

Marko and his latest orphanage find had started to dance, Griet noticed. And Anton and Petra had obviously decided it didn't matter that they didn't know each other from Adam. Griet's eyes swayed with Anton's hands on her sister's hips. No, decided Griet, Petra didn't need a warning. Petra had probably been born with more street sense that her sister would ever achieve.

Then she became aware of Sandra, standing beside her silently. Sandra was a small woman, even smaller than her brother's girlfriend, with the sort of helpless air that instantly transformed Griet into an efficient class captain.

'How about a drink? Have you had something to eat?'

'More than enough, thanks,' answered Sandra in her quiet voice.

Griet couldn't take her eyes off her sister's hips which were swaying ever more voluptuously under Anton's hands. She didn't know what to say to Sandra.

'Just look at my husband! Flirting again!' said Sandra like an indulgent mother of a mischievous child.

'Just look at my sister. Flirting again,' murmured Griet, like the awkward older sister she was.

'Just as long as he enjoys the evening,' said Sandra. 'He's working himself to death these days.'

'Well, it isn't as though you're exactly sitting at home loafing either, Sandra.'

'No, some days the children drive me up the wall,' she admitted with a radiant smile. She looked like Walt Disney's Snow White, gleaming black hair, rosy cheeks and baby-white skin. As though a singing dwarf would peep out from behind her skirt any moment, Griet always thought. 'It's such a pleasure to leave them with my mother sometimes and have a night out in town. You know how Anton loves a party. I enjoy just watching him enjoy himself!'

Could she really be that naïve? Or was she simply the

only kind of woman who'd always be happily married? She would either never know her husband was unfaithful, thought Griet, or never admit that she knew.

What if her own name had been Mary, thought Griet, not for the first time. Her life would undoubtedly have been different. She and her Joseph would probably still be together. Men just love rescuing women from difficulties, as Louise liked to say, and keeping the grateful woman in lifelong bondage. Mary couldn't very well leave Joseph, could she? Just as Snow White couldn't leave her prince. You can't walk away from a man who has literally rescued you from your own coffin.

It was the Gretels of the world who struggled with relationships, the girls who shoved the witch into the oven and rescued their brothers. It was they who made their wretched husbands impotent. If they ever found husbands.

If they ever wanted husbands.

Griet had been wondering about Hansel and Gretel for years. And the longer she thought about it, she had to admit, like Simonides, the further she apparently was from any answer.

'It's your turn,' said Marko, pulling her on to the patch of living-room floor where he was dancing. 'Do you remember teaching me how to slow dance?'

'I remember, and you thought I was crazy.'

'Well, I was still at school, Griet. What did you expect?'

'And you grew up to be the Fred Astaire of Cape Town.'

'Not for long. I'm off to Namibia next week.' He swung her under his arms before she could catch her breath and say something. 'I'm going to work for a foreign news agency.'

'To get away from the army?' she gasped.

'That's one of the reasons. But it's also an exciting place to be now. A new country.'

'But exciting things are happening here too . . .'

'They've got much further in Namibia. I don't want to hide from the army for another five years, Griet. I've had a gutful of hiding.' He twirled her under his arm again. 'I could already have a Namibian passport by then.'

She had to force herself to dance on. From early on she'd known Tienie would fly away as soon as she got the chance. And Petra had always been too ambitious to stay in one place. But Marko was her only brother.

'It's just so ... so sudden.' Oh, Hansel, Hansel, she thought, I'd push a witch into the oven for you. Even though she liked witches. 'Next week? Everything's happening too quickly.'

She'd lost too much. It was as though every man she loved disappeared from her life. Her grandfathers, her husband, her stepsons, her son ... and now her brother.

Except the father she couldn't talk to.

It felt as though she was cursed to live with women for ever. And men she couldn't talk to. And lovers who flapped their wings and flew away. And babies who only existed in her womb. And stories that only existed in her mind.

She tore herself out of her brother's arms and fled to the kitchen to get her emotions under control. She switched the microwave oven on because she didn't know what else to do; waited while the platter of snacks warmed up. She'd wrapped the oysters in bacon herself that morning, just as her mother always used to do for parties. And she'd actually enjoyed doing it.

It gradually came to her attention that she could hear a cricket chirping. It couldn't be, she thought incredulously. From cockroaches to crickets. Then she began to shake with silent laughter.

'And what's this standing in front of the oven laughing?'

Jans was in the kitchen door. He had his office clothes on, as usual, but he'd taken his jacket off and his tie hung over one shoulder. His eyes looked tired behind his spectacles. He was chewing an apple.

'I nearly forgot about you!' She battled to get her laughter under control.

'Better late than never,' he said apologetically. 'Like the so-called New South Africa.'

'No, I mean I nearly forgot that you're one of the few

men who . . .' The microwave oven pinged behind her and she turned to open the door. 'You've stood by me.'

'That smells heavenly.'

He sounded embarrassed, she realized as she turned back to him with the platter in her hands.

'They come from heaven. My mother calls them angels on horseback.'

'Tastes like heaven,' said Jans, popping one of the oyster-angels into his mouth. 'Did you make them?'

'Don't look so surprised.' Griet gave him the platter. 'Have another one.'

'Have a bite,' he said, giving her his half-eaten apple.

She looked at the apple. Golden Delicious. Sun gold on the outside, winter white inside.

'Do you know how much trouble the apple has already caused?'

'Well, there was the Apple of Eternal Youth in Scandinavian mythology,' said Jans, putting a second oyster into his mouth. 'The gods ate it to stay young. And there were various apples in Greek mythology. The Golden Apples of the Hesperides guarded by an eternally wakeful dragon with a hundred heads; the apples of Hippomenes . . .'

Griet laughed delightedly and took a bite of the apple. It was sweeter than she'd expected. Jans's eyes didn't look so tired any more.

'Now I remember,' she said. 'There was a good apple in the Arabian Nights too, one that could cure all ailments . . .'

'And of course there was the apple that unlocked the mysteries of gravity.'

'Newton's apple?' Griet's toes were tingling. That was always the first sign. 'I clean forgot about that. Maybe because I don't always believe in gravity.'

He'd always stood by her. Through thick and thin. Through divorce and death.

'Why have you never left me in the lurch, Jans?' The tingling was creeping up her legs and her stomach felt hollow. The second sign. 'Is there something wrong with you?'

'You make me laugh.'

Clever Griet makes the prince laugh! Her head was lighter than air. The third sign. She rose up, regally, grabbing at Jans below her. She rubbed his chin, the stubble like sandpaper under her fingers, her feet just clearing the floor. Then something happened that was so strange it could only have happened in a fairy tale. She saw his feet lift off the ground.

'Do you believe in happy endings?'

'No.' He looked confused by the unexpected attention. She could swear she felt the warmth of a blush on the cheek under her hand. He kissed her on the forehead. 'But you can always hope.'

He looked around nervously, as though he couldn't believe he was flying. Then his lips slid down to her ear.

'Am I imagining things,' he asked cautiously, 'or do I hear a cricket chirping?'